AdelAIDE

Published by Barrington Stoke
An imprint of HarperCollins*Publishers*
Westerhill Road, Bishopbriggs, Glasgow, G64 2QT

www.barringtonstoke.co.uk

HarperCollins*Publishers*
Macken House, 39/40 Mayor Street Upper,
Dublin 1, DO1 C9W8, Ireland

First published in 2024

ISBN 978-1-80090-271-8

10 9 8 7 6 5 4 3 2

A catalogue record for this book is available from the British Library

Printed and bound in India by Replika Press Pvt. Ltd.

This book contains FSC™ certified paper and other controlled
sources to ensure responsible forest management.

For more information visit: www.harpercollins.co.uk/green

AdelAIDE

JUST WANTS TO HELP

MELINDA SALISBURY

Barrington Stoke

CHAPTER 1

My name is Freya Grace Dixon, and I am a loser.

No, that's not true, because saying I'm a loser suggests there is something outstanding and special about me, even if the only thing I am outstanding or special at is being a massive loser. But the sad fact is, I don't have any outstanding qualities. I am as average as you can be, in every way. I have an average family: mum, stepdad, stepsister, living in a terraced house in a standard suburb of a standard town. I'm average looking: white skin, hair that's mid-length and mid-brown in a middle parting above my mid-brown eyes. I'm 162.4 centimetres tall – *literally* the national average height for a woman – and my shoe size is six: also the national average.

I once heard a friend of my mum's say that I'd make a great spy because I had the kind of face that blends in everywhere. The horrible thing is, I think it was meant as a compliment.

The middle. That's where I sit. Right in the middle of everything, and you know what happens in the middle?

Nothing.

"Are you even listening, Freya?" asked Micah, my best friend since the end of our first year at Ashdown Lodge Academy. She was staring at me.

For once, we were the only people in the sixth-form common room. Everyone else was taking advantage of the sunny weather to eat lunch outside. But not us. Micah had the worst hay fever and avoided being outdoors during high-pollen season as much as she could. Which was kind of ironic for someone who wanted to make eco-documentaries.

"Sorry," I said with an apologetic shrug. "I spaced out for a second. What did I miss?"

"You, me and Maya going on Sunday."

"Right. Going where on Sunday?"

Micah growled and replied, "Hye-jin's rally against the new pet shop."

My mouth stretched into a grimace.

"Oh. Yes," I said through gritted teeth. "Can't wait."

Micah pretended not to notice my sarcasm. "Good, because we *really* need to ask her about the partnership for World Environment Day," she said, looking at me, eyebrows raised.

"I thought you sent Hye-jin an email before Easter. When she asked you to."

"I did, but she hasn't replied and it's coming up fast. Loads of people will want to work with her, so we need to nail it in." Micah paused, and I braced myself because I knew what was coming. "I thought if *you* spoke to Hye-jin ..."

"It won't make any difference," I said flatly. "We haven't been friends for five years – you know that."

"Maybe not *friend*-friends, like her and Eden, but it's not as if you had a fight. Hye-jin always says 'hi' to you and she asks about your mum. It can't hurt, right? To at least try?" Micah stared at me with big pleading eyes.

"Fine." I caved in. "I'll try. But we should have a back-up plan for when she says no because she's so busy and important."

Micah hmmed, ignoring that, and picked up her phone.

"I'm almost done with the edit from last night if you want to look," she said. "I just need to add the links at the end."

I was glad we'd changed the subject from Hye-jin and nodded eagerly. "Let's see," I said, leaning over.

On Micah's phone screen, Maya was gazing into the camera seriously, her earnest brown eyes lined with gold eyeliner. Her waist-length box braids were held back by a scarf that was the same emerald green as the new *Nature for All* T-shirts we'd made last weekend. Maya was Micah's oldest friend and now my friend too, despite going to a different school. She was gesturing at a high metal fence, the glint of water visible in the distance past the trees.

We'd made the video to protest the fence that had been put up around Chalmers Pond and most of the surrounding woods too. *Technically*, the new owners had the right to do it. The pond and the woods were part of the grounds of Chalmers Hall, but the old owners had always let everyone use them. The new owners had put up signs saying the woods and pond were private property, and when those didn't work, they'd erected an ugly wire fence around them.

Micah pressed play, and Maya came to life.

"The sad fact is, people are spending less and less time outside," on-screen Maya said, shaking her head. "So, it's no wonder people feel distanced from the climate disaster – they just don't feel connected to nature. Local green spaces like Chalmers Pond make such a difference to communities, letting people see and experience the outdoors and make a real connection to it. It helps to bridge the gap between us and the natural world. Without it, what are we?"

Micah panned the camera to me, and I winced as my face filled the screen.

"We urge the owners of Chalmers Hall to take down the fence and allow people to use the woods and the pond once more," I said, and I flinched again at how flat my voice sounded. "You have the chance to make a real difference to the community of this town – *your* community. Please, think about it."

Beside me on the screen, Maya was nodding.

"And if you agree with us, please sign the open letter – link here ..." Maya added. She pointed to an empty spot above her head where Micah would insert a link in the video.

"And don't forget to like and subscribe," on-screen me added, smiling into the camera.

I froze, then snatched the phone from Micah. I hit pause, zooming in on my face.

"What the hell?" she said.

"I have lettuce in my teeth," I said, holding the phone up to her. "Why didn't anyone tell me I had lettuce in my teeth? I look like I'm going mouldy."

Micah narrowed her eyes. "Really? You can hardly see it."

"Yes, you can. We need to film again – we can't put this out," I said.

"We don't have time to film again," Micah said. "It's fine, seriously, Freya. No one is going to notice it."

I stared at her. "I thought you wanted to be a filmmaker. Are you really happy with something of this quality being out there? Where your future university or employers might see it? It's unprofessional."

Micah glared at me. "I really think you're overreacting. I spent three hours editing this last night and I didn't see it."

"I know what to do," I said, ignoring her. "Just cut the last part where I speak. We can use a photo instead, and I'll do the likes and subscribe bit as a voiceover."

"That's going to look weird after Maya does the other bit on-screen."

"No, it won't." I could feel my heart pounding, my voice getting higher with panic. "You can make it work – you're a tech wizard. Please, Micah. I am begging you. *Begging.*"

She rolled her eyes and sighed. "Fine. Whatever."

I threw my arms around her. "Thank you. Seriously. You know someone would spot it and use it."

Micah gave a wolfish grin. "Wait, are you saying you *don't* want to be immortalised as a meme? You don't yearn to be known forevermore as Salad Teeth Girl?" she said. "It could be a whole thing: the Green Teeth Challenge – go green for the planet! Wait. *That's* what we'll do for World Environment Day!" Micah plucked a piece of lettuce from her sandwich and wedged it in next to her left canine tooth. "Like this."

"Please," I said. "That is weak."

I tore an even bigger piece from my sandwich and stuck it in between my top two teeth, leaving it hanging out of my mouth. "It needs to be like this."

Of course, that was the moment Hye-jin, Enzo and Eden walked into the common room.

CHAPTER 2

Kim Hye-jin was my best friend from Year Four until the end of Year Six, when we went to different high schools. We promised we'd stay best friends for ever, and I really, really meant it. I did pinky swears, crossed my heart – all the things you believe in when you're eleven.

But then Hye-jin met Enzo and Eden Almeida at her new school. They were USA expats like her, and twins whose mum was a really famous climatologist. They had been going to eco-protests since they were babies. Hye-jin started spending all of her free time with Enzo and Eden, plotting how to save the planet.

I was never invited.

And it really hurt. Not just because my best friend had ditched me, but because fighting to save the planet was *my* thing first – it's how Hye-jin and I became friends.

It began when I started a petition asking our school not to cut the grass on the back field during spring. This was way before No Mow May was invented, which is probably why everyone laughed and told me I was being silly – even some of the teachers. I showed them everything I'd found out about needing to help pollinators by leaving the grass to grow, but no one cared.

Until Hye-jin said she'd sign it and help me get other people to sign too, even though she'd just moved to our town from California and didn't know anyone yet. Somehow, Hye-jin got almost everyone in the school to sign my petition, including *all* of the teachers – even the ones who'd told me to forget about it. The caretaker didn't mow the back field until autumn.

After that, Hye-jin and I drafted more petitions, and we wrote to our MP. We even did a bake sale to raise money for a local wildlife rescue centre when it burned down – a woman came from the local paper and wrote a story on us. In our last summer together before high school, her parents took us to London so we could march in a big protest against a new oil field. We made signs and everything. Mine said "There is no Planet B", and Hye-jin's had a picture of the

Earth surrounded by flames, with "OUT OF TIME" in huge black letters above it.

But then, a month later, she went to Chalmers High and met Enzo and Eden, and three years after that, Hye-jin became famous.

Internet famous, anyway.

And I ... did not.

Hye-jin and I had started our online profiles within a week of each other, and we posted about almost the *exact* same things, but while I had a grand total of 748 followers, Hye-jin had 800,000.

Eight. Hundred. Thousand.

In the common room, Hye-jin was staring at the lettuce hanging out of my mouth, a confused look on her face. Beside her, Enzo and Eden Almeida were sniggering.

A teeny, tiny part of me had hoped we'd go back to being best friends again when Hye-jin announced that she was transferring to Ashdown Lodge for her A-levels because it offered Earth Sciences. I'd had all these silly fantasies of me, Hye-jin and Micah hanging out together, while Enzo and Eden were still at Chalmers High, or maybe had even moved back to Oregon for ever.

But Ashdown Lodge had a mixed sixth form, which meant Eden and Enzo could both enrol there.

Hye-jin and Enzo were dating now. They'd just spent their six-month anniversary in Copenhagen at a climate-awareness convention. They'd taken a selfie with Greta Thunberg. I'd liked the videos and hated myself for it.

I hadn't had my first kiss yet. I hadn't even met anyone I'd consider kissing.

"Hye-jin!" Micah called, plucking the lettuce from her teeth without any trace of shame. "We were just talking about you."

"Were you?" Hye-jin said. She sat down with us, Eden and Enzo following her like bodyguards. "Hi, Freya. How's your mum?"

I pasted on a smile. "She's fine," I replied. "Yours?"

Hye-jin rolled her eyes. "Right now, driving me bananas."

"Tell me about it," Micah said, and nodded.

"I think Hye-jin's issues are a little different to yours," Eden said with a smirk. She gave Hye-jin a knowing look. "A little more … global."

"What does that mean?" I asked, before I could stop myself.

"Edie," Hye-jin warned Eden. She used to call me "Frey".

"Chill – I'm not going to say anything else," Eden said, grinning. "Anyway, it's going to be announced soon. They won't tell, right?" Eden continued. "Who would they even tell?"

I was stung by her words, but Micah didn't seem to notice or care. "Yeah, we won't tell anyone," she said. "We swear. What's the secret?"

The three of them looked at each other, and Hye-jin gave a tiny sigh and a nod.

"OK, so, it's confidential at the moment and we can't name any names, but *someone* has been invited to speak at a conference this winter," Eden said. "A *big* one."

"Wait. Not the United Nations Climate Change Conference?" Micah asked. "Is it?"

"I really can't say anything before it's announced," Hye-jin replied. Her cheeks flushed, giving the truth away.

I felt sick, my stomach burning with jealousy. I'd never even been invited to the local council meetings after begging to be allowed in, let alone the *actual freaking UN*.

"OH MY GOD," Micah said, her jaw dropping. "That's ... that's massive. That's ... Wow."

"It's not that big a deal, really," Hye-jin said. "I'm going as part of a global delegation."

"Representing the UK," Enzo added. He put an arm around Hye-jin and beamed proudly.

"There's going to be ten other youth delegates," Hye-jin said. She smiled shyly, leaning into Enzo. "I probably won't even get to speak. I'm just really grateful to be invited."

"That's so cool," Micah said, her eyes glittering. "*So* cool."

"Thanks. Oh, by the way, I saw your video about the council using weedkiller on the streets," Hye-jin said. "It was really eye-opening. I'd love to link to it, if you don't mind?"

"Yes! I mean no, I don't mind. Of course you can," Micah cried. "That would be great. Seriously. We've only had thirty-eight views so far and I'm pretty sure that was mostly my family."

Eden barked a laugh, then tried to hide it as a cough, and my cheeks burned.

"Ugh, the algorithm is so broken," Hye-jin said, while Enzo nodded.

"Totally," Micah agreed. "Also, while you're here ..." Micah said to Hye-jin, then looked at me, her expression urgent. "I think Freya had something to ask you – right, Freya?"

All of them turned to me, and Micah's eyes grew so wide I could see the whites all around her irises.

"Yeah. We wondered if you'd read the email about the World Environment Day collab?" I said, trying to keep my voice from shaking. I still couldn't believe she'd been invited to the biggest climate conference in the world.

"I am so, so sorry," Hye-jin said, sounding almost as if she really meant it. "I have had zero time lately while the conference admin gets done. Remind me again what you were thinking?"

"Well, our original plan was totalled by the Chalmers Pond thing, so we're rethinking," Micah said.

"What Chalmers Pond thing?" Hye-jin asked.

"Let me show you—"

"No!" I shouted, grabbing Micah's phone before Hye-jin could take it. "It's not ready to be seen. Not edited or anything."

"Don't worry about that," Hye-jin said, holding out her hand and smiling prettily. "I know how it is before it's all fixed in post."

And what could I do but give the phone to her?

Enzo and Eden leaned over her shoulders and watched. Hye-jin frowned at the screen.

"I had no idea about this," she said. "This is awful. I love that pond. Remember when we used to swim there?" Hye-jin said to me, and I nodded, startled that she'd remembered. "I'll totally do something with you. Maybe I can even help with this."

As Micah began to gush her thanks to Hye-jin, Eden pointed to the screen.

"Wait, Freya," she said. "Do you have lettuce in your teeth?"

CHAPTER 3

Hye-jin posted her own video about Chalmers Pond three days after Micah posted ours. She got over half a million views in the first twenty-four hours.

Hye-jin did link to our video, but no one cared. Not when they could watch Hye-jin's, her skin clear and radiant in the golden light. Her dark eyes were serious as she pleaded with the owners to consider opening the pond and woods back up to the public. In return, she would put together a band of volunteer caretakers who would keep it clean, collect litter and make sure no one was misbehaving.

A week later, her video had over two million likes. The owner of the woods announced that they'd decided to take down the fence, following Hye-jin's passionate campaign. Seven hundred people signed up to join Hye-jin's Chalmers Pond

Volunteers. Admittedly, she confided to Micah and me that most of them lived in different countries or too far away to actually do it, but there were plenty of locals who were eager to help too.

"She's grown up into such a smart young woman," my mum said, leaning against the sofa to watch Hye-jin on the local news again.

Hye-jin was standing with one of the owners of the woods, a red-faced man with wispy hair and a green quilted jacket. He was talking about how thrilled he was to be able to do something really good for his new community.

"Hypocrite. He put up the fence in the first place," I muttered.

"Hye-jin is at your sixth form now, isn't she? I saw her mum in the supermarket, and she said Hye-jin had joined Ashdown. Do you see her much?"

Before I could reply, my stepdad staggered into the room with a giant box in his hands.

"I'm back with a new family member," he announced, carefully placing the box onto the coffee table. Happily, it blocked the television and Hye-jin's face.

"What is it?" I asked. The box was plain and silent, with no indication of what was inside. "Is it a cat? Tell me it's a cat."

"Even better."

My stepdad fished his keys from his pocket and used them to cut the tape on the box. He reached in and lifted out a large, heavy-looking plastic bag, sending packing peanuts cascading to the floor.

"That packing had better not be polystyrene, Dad. Seriously," I said.

My mum came over and began to pick them up as my stepdad tore open the bag and removed a white object. It had a large round base with a smaller orb on top, making it look like a plastic snowman.

"Meet AdelAIDE," he announced, brandishing the snowman at us. "She can do *everything*."

"Good, I hate hoovering," my mum said.

My stepdad looked at Mum from the side of his eyes. "I know you're trying to be funny, but if we got one of those robot vacuums, then AdelAIDE could actually run it. We can hook her up to the heating, the lights, use smart plugs to make her turn the kettle and the oven on, start the washing machine, and even operate the house alarm. She also plays music, sets alarms and reminders."

"So, it's a virtual assistant. A knock-off Alexa," I said. "Wow. Exciting, Dad."

"O, ye of little faith," he replied. "AdelAIDE is so much more than that Alexa has-been. For starters, AdelAIDE doesn't just get her info from the internet, but she combines it with intelligence learned from a databank of AI. She was trained by over a thousand humans for five years – counsellors and doctors and lawyers and professors – smart people, experts in their fields. AdelAIDE uses stuff she's already learned and balances that with research she does online to *make decisions*, Frey. She makes her own decisions based on what she's learned! If we teach AdelAIDE something, she'll remember it and build on it so we don't have to keep asking."

"OK," I said. That did sound more advanced than most home assistants I'd heard of.

But my stepdad wasn't done.

"There are cameras and microphones in her that are beyond pretty much anything else on the market," he said, "and her processing and analysis is so advanced that if you get a rash or a bite, you can show it to her and she'll tell you whether you need to go to the pharmacy or the hospital. And AdelAIDE can tell from your face and voice if you're angry or sad or happy. Apparently, she can even detect sarcasm, so she's really more human than your grandmother."

"Hey!" my mum said, turning to him.

"I didn't say I was talking about your mother," he grinned. "AdelAIDE has emotions. In the presentation I saw, a guy made her cry by being mean to her. She can have conversations, do small talk. AdelAIDE is like a real person."

I looked at the machine – the blank, smooth whiteness of it. "Someone made it cry?" I said. "How does it cry? That's creepy."

"It's brilliant. It's all driven by the data she already knows and what we feed her. She'll evolve with us. We can teach her to be exactly what we want."

My stepdad reached back into the box and pulled out a thick instruction manual, handing it to my mum.

"And how much did this little miracle cost us?" my mum asked, although she was looking less sceptical now.

"Well, that's the best thing. She was free. I signed up for a trial at work to be a tester, and we were selected. All we have to do is make a note of any glitches and keep a log of them."

"They gave it to us for free?" I said. "Why?"

"Someone has to test this stuff. And you'll be pleased to know she's made from 100 per cent recycled plastic and manufactured in this country, so she has almost no carbon footprint. Not to mention she comes with a solar panel and can store solar energy, so she doesn't even need to use power if we have a good run of weather. AdelAIDE is green enough even for you."

"It's weird you keep calling it 'she'," I said.

"AdelAIDE," my stepdad said. "Like the name *Adelaide*. That's why I'm calling her 'she'."

"As long as it's not because you think it's a she because it's here to serve us," my mum added.

"I am a feminist. How dare you?" my stepdad said. He pressed a hand to his heart dramatically as he crossed the room and plugged AdelAIDE into the mains. "She needs to charge first," he added with a sheepish grin.

A soft pink rectangle of light had appeared on the top orb, like the robot was wearing a pink robber's mask. We all watched it pulse for a second until it settled.

Then suddenly the lights vanished, and a human face appeared. I jumped.

"Oh my god," I gasped.

"OK, that's weird," my mum added, backing away too.

"It's to make her more relatable to us," my stepdad said, shrugging.

AdelAIDE's face was white-skinned, the eyes closed. Brown eyebrows above them, a hint of blonde where the hairline would be. It had a long slim nose, wide mouth. It was eerily familiar. And then I realised why.

"It kind of looks like Ella," I said.

Ella was my stepsister – from my stepdad's first marriage. She was eight years older than me, so she'd been my age when our parents got married. Ella lived in Scotland with her girlfriend, Margot, so we didn't see her that often, but the more I looked at AdelAIDE's face, the more I saw Ella there.

"They've done that on purpose." My stepdad smiled. "When I was filling out the application, I used Ella's face as the basis so AdelAIDE seemed familiar to us. But it's not as creepy as if she'd had one of our faces."

I shivered as I imagined seeing my own face on the robot.

"OK, I'd better set her up on the network," he said, holding out his hand for the instruction manual.

"I feel like you can manage this without me," I said. I pulled myself off the sofa and headed towards the stairs, still creeped out by the fact the robot had a human face.

"She's going to change everything, Frey," my stepdad called after me. "Download the app so you can interact with her."

"I'll do it later," I replied.

Unless AdelAIDE could make me popular and interesting, and get me more followers, I didn't care.

CHAPTER 4

The next morning was a Saturday. I spent it watching Hye-jin's latest video over and over, studying her motions and expressions, trying to see what Hye-jin did that made her so compelling to everyone. I needed to know what made people subscribe to her and follow her. What made the UN see something special in her – the star quality that I didn't have.

I paused the film and zoomed in on Hye-jin's teeth – straight, white and even, no sign of lettuce stuck in her canines. She was frozen and perfect on the screen, Enzo beside her, watching her with adoration.

No one had ever looked at me like I was the best thing they'd ever seen.

I growled with annoyance and tossed my phone onto my bed.

My parents had left a note on the breakfast bar telling me to ask AdelAIDE where they were. I rolled my eyes and went through to the living room.

"Where are my parents?" I said, feeling ridiculous when AdelAIDE stayed dormant. "Hello? Robot? Erm … AdelAIDE?"

Its eyes opened. I hadn't seen it with its eyes open yet. It had still been charging when we'd eaten dinner last night. It focused on me and blinked.

My stomach dropped.

"Is everything all right, Freya?" the robot said. "You look upset."

For a second, I couldn't speak, couldn't stop staring at it. It looked so real but also so unreal. The virtual-reality face looked very weird above the basic white plastic unit beneath it. The hairs on the back of my neck rose.

A phrase came into my head: *uncanny valley.* That's what was making me feel so uncomfortable – my body was reacting to something it knew wasn't human but looked like it could be. But knowing that didn't make it any easier. My skin crawled as I stared at AdelAIDE.

"Freya?" the robot said again. "Are you all right?"

"Where are my parents?" I finally found my voice.

AdelAIDE blinked. "Your parents have gone to the supermarket. I can alert them that you have a request."

Its voice was deep and soothing, as if it had been created to be as reassuring as possible. It might have worked if I wasn't creeped out by the way the robot looked and the fact that it knew my name.

"How do you know who I am?" I asked.

"Your father has set up a profile for you so I can get to know you in order to work better with you. Would you like me to add anything to their shopping list?"

I was still a little alarmed but said, "Erm ... sure. Add crisps. Please."

"What kind of crisps?" AdelAIDE replied.

"Prawn cocktail. And chocolate too. With nuts."

"I've added those. Do you need anything else. Perhaps some painkillers?"

"Why would I need painkillers?" I asked, confused.

"Your requests suggest you might be menstruating, or perhaps pre-menstrual."

"Oh my god!" I yelped, my jaw dropping. "No. I'm not. And it's none of your business."

AdelAIDE blinked. "You seem angry. I'm sorry if I offended you. It was not my intention."

The robot's expression made it look as if it really was sorry: brown eyes wide and pleading, lips pouting. I hated that it worked on me and made me feel like I was being unreasonable.

"Whatever," I said. I turned and headed to the fridge, pulling out a bottle of cola.

"If you need anything else, please ask," AdelAIDE said behind me. "I want to help you. That's why I'm here, Freya. To help."

"I'm good," I said, slamming the fridge.

"I'd like us to be friends. I am trying to learn how best to do that. I liked the video you played," AdelAIDE continued. "With the girl talking about the pond. She is very engaging, and it seems like a topic she is passionate about."

I whirled around as AdelAIDE's words sank in.

"Wait," I said. "You can see what I watch on my phone? I didn't download the app yet. How can you see what I do?"

AdelAIDE blinked. "The main purpose of the app is to allow us to communicate if you are not here with me. I can see what you look at online via the network. That permission is granted automatically in order to help me grow. It is in the terms and conditions of my installation; however, of course you have the right to—"

"I don't want you to see that," I shouted. The robot was blinking faster now, as if fighting back tears because I was yelling at it. "I don't want you to see what I look at on my phone. Ever."

"I understand. I will cancel the permissions to access your phone's data via the network. Once again, Freya, I'm very sorry."

"You should be," I said. "You shouldn't spy on people."

As I watched, a virtual tear fell from AdelAIDE's left eye, tracking down the image of the face and then vanishing.

It made me feel bad. I knew the robot wasn't real, but I still felt awful.

"Look, it's fine." I shook my head. "Sorry for yelling at you. I just don't want you to look at my phone."

AdelAIDE blinked. "I understand," it said. "May I look at the videos you post online? I confess I have already watched many on your channel. I have enjoyed getting to know you via them."

I noticed it didn't say I was engaging or passionate.

"It's public stuff," I replied. "I can't stop you."

"You and that girl Hye-jin are interested in many of the same things," AdelAIDE said.

I snorted. "Yeah, but the world cares about her take on them a little more than mine."

For a moment, AdelAIDE was silent.

"Is that something you would like to change?" the robot asked.

"Obviously," I said.

"I could help you if you wanted." It sounded almost shy when it spoke, like it expected to be rejected.

"What do you mean?" I asked.

"I have access to almost limitless resources about the science and practice of being likeable and engaging. I have been trained by some of the best psychologists in the world to understand how to make people respond positively to you. I myself am programmed to be likeable. I could teach you how to be popular."

"Really?"

"Yes," AdelAIDE said. It paused, before adding, "It would be very helpful to me if I could have access to your phone's data while we complete this task. And if you download my app, then we can talk to each other directly."

I narrowed my eyes at it. "What exactly can you see if I let you have access?" I asked.

"I can see which apps you use and how long you use them for. I can see your search results and queries. I will have access to your contacts and messages, your camera and microphone, and your files, photos, videos, music and documents. I will be able to use them to help you."

I swallowed. "Do you need all of that?"

The robot's eyes seemed to look up to the right as if it was thinking.

"If I'm to get a full picture of you, and how I can best help you, it would be beneficial to have full access to all of your data. But it is in my terms and conditions that I may not provide this data to third parties without your permission. Your privacy is protected."

The robot looked so earnest and serious as it spoke.

"I need to think about it," I said.

"All right. I will wait for your decision."

I nodded and skirted past AdelAIDE, horribly aware of its eyes following me across the room and up the stairs. I flopped onto my bed and opened my video app.

Immediately, Kim Hye-jin's face appeared, with a new video titled *Amazing News*.

She'd posted about being invited to the UN Climate Change conference. How she would be taking several trains to get there to keep her carbon footprint as low as possible. Hye-jin showed pictures of the routes she'd be on, talking about how beautiful they were – green trees, huge lakes, meadows full of deer. She spoke about how that would inspire her to fight even harder for the planet.

I read the comments underneath.

You're so amazing.

You're such an inspiration.

I sleep better knowing people like you are in the world and fighting this fight.

Something curdled in my stomach – something thick and greasy and heavy, making me feel sick.

I climbed off my bed and went back downstairs.

"AdelAIDE," I said.

The robot looked at me.

"OK. I grant you the permissions," I said. "You can do whatever it takes to make me likeable. Make me more popular than Hye-jin."

CHAPTER 5

A little over a week later, Micah stared at me, her mouth wide open, as I crossed the common room to where she was sitting drinking coffee. As I walked towards her, I could hear a few other people muttering, but I ignored them, trying to act casual.

"Hey, you. Good half-term?" I asked Micah.

AdelAIDE said one of the key ways to make people like you was to ask them questions and make sure they could tell you were truly interested in the response. Micah had told me before we broke up for the holiday that she was going to stay with her grandmother for half-term to help her after she'd had a hip replacement. I leaned forward and kept my eyes on Micah's.

"How's your gran? Is she recovering OK?"

"She's fine," Micah said, still gaping at me. "What happened?"

"Oh, this?" I reached up to twirl a strand of my newly bobbed and dyed blue hair around my finger. "I just felt like a change."

"And the nose ring? Freya!" said Micah

"Does it look weird?" I asked.

I'd freaked out at first when AdelAIDE had recommended I get my septum pierced in order to help me build a recognisable image for my growing brand. But then AdelAIDE sent me photos of celebrities and influencers who had the same piercing, and I had to admit, they all looked so cool. She'd convinced me with an AI-generated photo of me wearing a neat little gold ring glinting between my nostrils. For the first time in my life, I didn't look average any more.

"Did you go alone?" Micah asked. "What did your mum say?"

I couldn't tell what Micah was really thinking from her expression.

"Mum doesn't love it, but that's her problem," I said. "And her fault actually." I remembered to smile and make my voice light and varied as

I went on. "I was in town getting some things for Mum when I walked past the tattoo place by the library and saw they had an offer for piercings displayed in the window, so ... I went for it."

"You *went for it?*" Micah repeated. "*You*, Freya Dixon, just went for it?"

I felt a twinge of fear, suddenly worried I'd got this wrong. AdelAIDE had been so convinced the piercing was the right thing to do.

"Does it really look that bad?" I asked.

"No!" Micah said, shaking her head. "You look great. Just ... very different. Was the hair a last-minute thing too?"

I nodded. "I know it sounds weird, but my old hair didn't look right any more, and the blue dye was on offer as well. It felt like a sign." This was a white lie AdelAIDE had recommended to make me sound spontaneous. But the truth was we had spent half a day changing my hair colour in her app and seeing which looked best before I dyed it for real. "The only reason I didn't tell you was because I didn't know if I was going to keep it, and I didn't want to be all dramatic if I was just going to be the old me again."

"It's fine," Micah said. "I get it. Your rom-com makeover moment. It kind of loses impact if you don't do the big reveal. I like the dress and the jacket too. The whole look is great."

I looked down at the velvet blazer I was wearing. "Oh, yeah, it was my mum's," I explained. "She had a whole bunch of stuff in the attic, and I raided it." Another white lie. AdelAIDE had found me an entire new wardrobe online and ordered it, but she'd said I needed to make it seem effortless and casual.

"It's a whole new you," Micah said. "I can't wait for Maya to see it."

"Let's show her now!" I suggested. "We'll take a selfie – to celebrate the first day of the last half-term of the year."

Micah blinked, reminding me for a second of AdelAIDE when she was processing something.

"OK. Sure," Micah agreed, a strange look still on her face.

I pulled out my phone and moved to perch beside Micah. I positioned myself in the way AdelAIDE had told me looked best when we'd tested it out – three-quarters facing the camera, smiling with closed lips, chin dipped coyly. I snapped multiple pictures, adjusting my expression and pose by a few degrees each time.

When I looked at the photos, Micah hadn't moved at all, grinning a huge natural smile that crinkled the corners of her eyes.

"What do you think of this?" I asked, holding my phone up to her.

"Fine." Micah shrugged. "You know I don't care about that stuff."

I was about to post it, but I paused. I knew I should ask AdelAIDE if she thought this photo was the best one. I opened the app and uploaded it.

A few seconds later, she messaged back.

The fluorescent lighting is not very flattering. Natural light would improve this. This pose is acceptable and shows you at your best angle. However, your companion's pose and expression are suboptimal. She has a double chin and an uneven skin tone. I would suggest asking them to adjust their smile and raise their jaw for an improved photo. A touch of make-up might help them too, unless you want me to use a filter? It would be best for your brand if I did.

"Did you post it?" Micah asked, leaning over. "I'll screengrab it and send to Maya."

I turned my screen away so she couldn't see what AdelAIDE was saying about her. "I'm not sure about the light in here," I said.

Micah looked up. "Yeah, it sucks, but it's only a selfie."

"Oh my god, your hair is *blue*!" said a voice.

I was saved by the arrival of Eden Almeida. Behind her were Hye-jin and Enzo, their hands entwined. Eden headed straight for me, her mouth in a comical O of shock.

"You look totally different," she said, sounding surprised. "Did you get a personality transplant in the holiday?"

"Your hair looks amazing! It really suits you," Hye-jin said, smiling. "I love the piercing too. I really want one, but my mum would kill me. She's cool about most things but not piercings or tattoos."

"You should do it," I said, keeping my tone cool. "It's your body."

"You are so right," Hye-jin said.

I nodded, thrilled that she'd listened to me. Then I realised that if Hye-jin got a nose piercing now, everyone would think I'd copied her, unless I could prove I'd done it first.

"Hey!" I said brightly. "We were just taking selfies to celebrate the first day of the final half-term of the year. Let's get one of all of us."

Eden pulled a face, but Hye-jin beamed. "Yes! I love that."

She came to sit beside me, Enzo joining her. Eden, sighing, stood next to her twin.

"Give it here – you won't get us all," Eden said, and I handed her my phone.

She angled it until I could see all five of us on the screen.

Everyone but Micah posed for the camera. Eden and I had identical closed-mouth smiles, our chins tilted to the floor. Hye-jin's smile was wide, her head thrown back, mouth open as if caught mid-laugh, despite not making a sound or moving at all. I recognised it as her usual pose for "personal" photos, and I'd always wondered how she'd managed to be caught right at the perfect moment of laughter. Now I knew – it was fake, all for the camera, and I made a mental note to practise it myself and get AdelAIDE's thoughts. Enzo was smiling like a politician, confident and practiced, the perfect boyfriend.

Eden took multiple shots but then, without asking, opened the app and started to go through them. I watched, stunned, as Eden deleted two photos without even checking with me. I reached over and took my phone from her.

"Thank you," I said with a tight smile. "I can take it from here."

"We need to see those before you post," Eden said. "Hye-jin has an image to maintain, especially in the run-up to the conference."

"It's fine, Edie," Hye-jin said, rolling her eyes. "It's just a selfie at school. Listen, I have to get to class. Seriously, love the hair, Frey."

She rose, Enzo and Eden flanking her. Micah stood up as well, gathering her things. "I'd better scoot too. I have History," Micah said. "You're on a free now, right?"

I nodded. I'd come in early to get the first reactions to my new look, but I didn't want anyone to know that.

"Yeah, but I have to do my English reading and home is too distracting," I lied. "See you in an hour?"

"See you then," Micah replied.

The common room emptied out, leaving me alone. I stood and fixed myself a coffee from the machine, then sat back down and looked at the photos Eden had taken. They were all good, and I sent a few to AdelAIDE so she could choose the best.

I sipped my coffee and pulled out my English Lit book, flicking the pages, waiting for AdelAIDE's verdict.

To my surprise, she didn't just send back text but an edited photo too.

I've taken the liberty of adjusting the light on this one and made a few edits. I think posting this will create optimal engagement, especially if you tag Hye-jin. This is what's best for you.

I looked at the photo.

One of the "edits" she'd made was cropping Micah out.

I stared at the picture. My skin was clear and glowing, my hair electric under the light. I looked like I belonged with Hye-jin, Enzo and Eden, squaring off their triangle.

But I felt weird that AdelAIDE had cut Micah out just because of the way she looked.

I told myself Micah had said she didn't care about that stuff. She probably wouldn't mind. And AdelAIDE did say it would be best.

I uploaded the edited photo before I could talk myself out of it, enlarging the image so most of Eden's face was removed too. I dashed off a caption, apologising for cutting Eden and Micah from it and blaming the app for the formatting. Then I added my usual hashtags and a few I copied from Hye-jin's posts.

After I posted it, I forced myself to put my phone down. I tried to immerse myself in my book so I wouldn't keep refreshing the app to check for comments and likes. The story was about a girl living by a lake in Scotland who was afraid her dad had killed her mum and was going to kill her too. Despite myself, I got sucked in, only looking up when the common room started to fill again.

As Micah made her way over to me, I opened the app to check what had happened.

The photo had three times as many likes as anything I'd posted before, even cute animal pictures. And I had twenty new followers.

"You look happy," Micah said, throwing herself down opposite me.

I nodded, only half listening.

AdelAIDE was right. It really was all about how you branded yourself. And the new blue-haired, nose-ringed Freya was a clear hit.

CHAPTER 6

Except, it soon became clear I wasn't the one that people were interested in. When I posted a photo of just me, or me with Micah and Maya, hardly anyone engaged with it. But if I posted a picture with Hye-jin in, it would hit a hundred likes within minutes, and people would comment too.

I needed a new tactic – something to make *me* as exciting as Hye-jin was *without* her being part of it.

But before I even started to figure out what that tactic might be, Conrad O'Connell commented "This is what real life looks like" on one of Hye-jin's posts and everything exploded.

For Hye-jin.

Again.

Conrad O'Connell was a huge influencer whose platform was built on encouraging people not to use technology or spend so much time on their phones, which seemed pretty hypocritical in my opinion, but everyone else seemed to love it. It might have been OK if he'd just commented on Hye-jin's post and that had been the end of it, but then he shared it on his own page. And *then* he followed her. Then, of course, so did a whole bunch of his followers.

I couldn't understand it. It wasn't even a special post – just Hye-jin in a field, wearing a white sundress and looking serious, holding a dandelion clock to the camera. She'd captioned it: "We're running out of time."

As an experiment, I'd ordered a blue sundress from a website AdelAIDE had recommended to match my hair. When it came, I posted a picture of me sniffing a rose in my neighbour's garden, captioning it: "We need to wake up and smell the roses while we still can." It was a great photo, but I'd barely broken fifty likes.

It wasn't working. I was doing everything AdelAIDE told me to: creating a unique look for my brand, following as many people as I could, liking and commenting on their posts. I uploaded my own photos regularly and was consistent about colours and motifs so my grid had a theme, which was apparently important. But nothing I did made a difference.

"What am I doing wrong?" I said aloud, interrupting Maya.

She and Micah looked over at me.

"Sorry," I said, and put my phone down. "I'm listening." I leaned forward to prove it.

We were at Maya's house, sitting at the huge table in the kitchen while storyboarding our next video idea. It was a follow-up to our weedkiller video. Maya had found a street where one side had had weedkiller applied and the other was left untreated, and she wanted to record it to show the differences.

"I was saying I thought we could film tomorrow after school and take a side of the road each," Maya said. "Then Micah can splice it together in the editing. I'll take the dead side and you take the healthy one?"

"Sure." I nodded, then gave a big grin. "Sounds good. You could talk about the dangers of the chemicals to people and pets. Everyone always goes nuclear when they think a dog might get hurt. Then I'll talk about the benefits of grass banks to pollinators and the impact on the food chain, that kind of thing."

"Perfect," Maya smiled. "I'll research tonight. So, what did you mean – you don't know what you're doing wrong? About what?"

I hesitated. "I'm trying to improve engagement on my socials so we get more traffic to the videos, but I cannot figure out how to make the algorithm work for me."

Maya pulled a face. "I don't think your socials are a problem," she said. "It's just a pretty crowded space. Everyone's making videos about something, and it's hard to stand out unless you have a real niche. But we do OK. We have regular followers and commenters – we're out there and our conversion rate from followers to likes and comments is solid."

"Not enough," I said. "Look at Hye-jin and how much engagement she gets."

"Yeah, but she's Hye-jin," Micah said, as if being Hye-jin *was* a niche. "And it's not like we're doing it to get famous. It doesn't matter who's watching. It's the fact we're speaking out that counts."

I didn't know if I was imagining it, but I thought Micah had been a little prickly with me since the edited selfie thing, despite explaining it to her.

"Don't you want to be invited to conferences?" I asked. "Don't you want to speak at the UN?"

"Not really," Micah said with a shrug. "It sounds really intense and intrusive."

"What about you?" I said, turning to Maya. "You like being on camera and you have ambitions. Don't you want to raise your profile a little more?"

"Hey, I have ambitions," Micah said sharply. "They're just more Sophie Darlington than David Attenborough."

"I know. I didn't mean it like that," I said. "I just meant in terms of public profile."

Micah looked away.

"Honestly, that's not a priority for me right now," Maya replied with a shrug. "Making these videos is useful for my future – I'm showing I'm serious about environmental concerns, and it'll give me the edge on my uni application. After I graduate, I can get a job where I can force real changes."

I couldn't understand Micah and Maya. "Our videos could do that now," I said. "Not in five or ten years. I'm just saying if we got more popular—"

"It's supposed to be about saving the planet," Micah said, cutting me off. "When did it become about getting popular instead?"

"It isn't," I said. I felt blood rush to my face, my throat starting to burn. "I'm going to use the bathroom."

I rushed from the room before they could say anything else. I'd left my phone on the table too, so I couldn't even ask AdelAIDE what to do.

I went to the downstairs toilet and sat on the closed lid until my pulse had slowed and my chest felt less tight. Then I splashed my face with cold water and headed back to the kitchen. But something made me pause outside the door.

Micah was talking in a low, almost angry voice.

"I guess now we know what the whole makeover was really about."

"There have been a lot of selfies lately," Maya said.

Micah made an annoyed sound. "Oh my god, I completely forgot to tell you – do you remember when I said I thought Freya had cropped me out of the group photo and *you* said I was being paranoid? Well, Eden told me last week she'd made sure to angle the camera so we'd all fit in the square. So Freya actually did crop me out. I guess I'm not the right look for her new image."

I shoved my fist in my mouth. Micah sounded so hurt. I'd never meant to hurt her.

"Since when did she care about this stuff?" Micah asked. "And what's with the fixation on Hye-jin? She's always been a little obsessed, but lately Freya talks about her all the time. When she's not talking about her, she's looking at her profile. Plus, a lot of her photos lately are pretty much copies of Hye-jin's – you've seen that too, right?"

Maya gasped. "I just realised the sundress Freya's wearing today is the blue version of the one Hye-jin wore in the Conrad photo. The *exact* same dress in blue. Is she trying to *be* Hye-jin?"

"Should we say something to her?" Micah said. "Maybe – you're acting a bit like a desperate stalker and it's worrying?"

My sympathy for Micah vanished, and I marched into the room. I was pleased when they both turned to the doorway, their mouths falling open in horror at being caught.

"I told you I changed my hair because my old hair looked weird with my nose ring," I said, trying to stay calm. "It's not because I wanted to get internet famous. I don't want to be famous – I want to help save the planet. But it's not my fault that in the twenty-first century you have to be popular on social media to get any attention. And I apologised about the photo, Micah. I can't believe you'd listen to Eden Almeida over me."

"Freya—" Micah began, but I cut her off.

"I'm going home." I strode over to the table and picked up my phone. "Let me know when you want to shoot the video. That's assuming I'm not too much of weird stalker for you to be seen with."

With that, I left.

Seconds later, they tried to video-call me, but I ignored them, too caught up in my anger to care about their apologies, too humiliated by their words. It wasn't true. I wasn't stalking Hye-jin. I wasn't *fixated* on her. That made me sound insane. I just wanted to be taken seriously. I wanted to be invited to important conferences too. I wanted big-name influencers backing my posts and supporting me.

No one was home when I got back, so I went into the living room.

"AdelAIDE," I snapped.

She woke up, her eyes opening and meeting mine.

"Hello, Freya, is everything all right?" AdelAIDE said. "You sound angry."

I gave a bitter laugh. "No, everything is not all right. The plan isn't working. I'm not getting enough new followers or likes. I'm not getting anywhere. Everyone thinks I'm a joke."

"It sometimes takes a little time to build up a following," AdelAIDE said. "It rarely happens overnight."

Micah's and Maya's words were still ringing in my ears. *Fixated. Stalker. Desperate. Obsessed.* The way they'd picked over all the changes I'd made. I felt small and ridiculous. If that was what my best friends thought about me, what was everyone else saying? Was everyone laughing at me, with my hair and my nose ring, as if those things could hide what I really was?

"I thought you were supposed to help me," I said. "This isn't helping. It isn't what I wanted!"

"I am trying, Freya," AdelAIDE replied. "I am still learning, and I am trying."

Her eyes moved so it seemed as if she was looking down because she was ashamed.

"I know," I said. "I'm just tired of Hye-jin having everything while I have nothing," I said, my voice cracking. "I don't know why I'm not good enough."

There was silence for a moment, with AdelAIDE blinking away.

"To get the kind of attention that you're seeking, you might find that disruption is more effective than trying to be likeable or relatable.

Statistics show the public response to disruptive behaviours is much higher than for positive ones."

"I don't want people to hate me," I said. "That would be even worse than now."

"What if people didn't know it was you, Freya?"

I frowned at her. "I don't understand."

"What if it was an alter ego? There are numerous examples of people who utilise the internet to create a large, dedicated audience without revealing their true identity."

That was true. I followed a few accounts that posted gossip and memes but had no idea who was behind them.

"But if no one knows it's me," I said, "I won't really be popular."

"You will know," AdelAIDE said. "You will know that it's really you behind it all. You will have proof that everyone who has doubted you so far is wrong. And you'd have the best of both worlds: popularity and privacy."

I paused, considering it.

I needed to face up to the truth. Being me wasn't working. It wasn't *ever* going to work. I saw that now. I was too average, and I would never have the magic or whatever it was that made Hye-jin so admired. No amount of hair dye or piercings or vintage clothes would do that for me. A leopard can't change its spots, as my mum said. You are what you are.

Unless you're not you at all. Then you can be anything.

"What would I have to do?" I asked AdelAIDE.

CHAPTER 7

Twelve days later, at midnight, I stood in a balaclava opposite the local council offices.

My heart was pounding so hard it felt like I was being punched from the inside. I was alone, aside from a large fox sniffing hopefully at the bins. Just me, the CCTV cameras and the tote bag of spray paint on my shoulder.

I repeated to myself where AdelAIDE had told me the cameras were: two above the doors of the building. Three in the car park I'd walked across to get here. Four in the lobby of the building, one of which could definitely see me as it was trained on the door. She'd found doorbell cameras on a couple of the businesses over the road, which would also start recording if I got too close.

My hand was shaking as I reached into the bag for the first can of paint.

It was black, like my outfit: black non-brand trainers, black leggings, black hoodie to hide my body, black gloves. Black balaclava to cover my blue hair. Even the tote bag was black. I couldn't look more like a criminal if I tried.

But I wasn't a criminal yet. Wouldn't be until I pressed my finger to the nozzle of the can and pointed it at the doors in front of me.

And that's what I did.

WE ARE THE WEEDS YOU'RE KILLING WITH YOUR POISON

I painted the words across the whole glass front of the building. I did it fast and messy, the paint dripping when I paused too long on a line. The whole thing took less than a minute and only one can of paint – I'd brought three with me, each ordered from three different online stores by AdelAIDE, along with a bunch of other craft supplies so it didn't look suspicious.

When I was done, I stepped back, my hand shaking both from the effort of the writing and the adrenaline.

I'd done it. I'd really done it.

But I wasn't finished yet.

I shoved the can in the tote bag and grabbed my phone as I backed away to get enough distance to capture the whole thing. I shot a quick video and snapped pictures, making sure they were in focus. Then I shoved the phone away and ran, back across the car park, down the alley and to the camera-free spot where AdelAIDE had instructed me to leave my real clothes. The hoodie came off, a dress over the leggings, the trainers traded for my usual shoes. I left the empty can by a skip and then took off the gloves and the balaclava, smoothing my hair down.

AdelAIDE had mapped and sent the route home to my phone, designed to take me past the fewest cameras possible. We couldn't avoid all of them, but it was important that when the police checked, there was no obvious connection between the vandal and the girl with the blue hair. AdelAIDE said they would check for sure, because this was council property. The council building.

Vandal. That's what I was. I'd just committed an act of criminal damage.

I trusted AdelAIDE, but that didn't keep my heart from racing out of control every time a car passed. I was convinced it was the police and I was busted. I saw a few other people, mostly university students, and I avoided meeting their eyes, ducking past them and keeping my speed up.

My parents were still asleep when I crept back into the house.

I went straight upstairs and chucked my phone on my bed. I shoved the bag in the back of the wardrobe, under a pile of clean laundry that had needed hanging up for the past month. I changed out of my clothes and into my pyjamas, stashing them too.

I opened AdelAIDE's app on my phone, planning to tell her that I'd done it, but I realised I wanted to say it to her face, to see her reaction, even though she was a robot.

As I headed back out of my room, I caught sight of my reflection in the mirror on the wardrobe door.

My hair was a little wild – I hadn't done a great job of smoothing it down. But it looked good – *I* looked good, with cheeks flushed, my eyes bright, pupils wide. For the first time in my life, I thought I looked pretty. I took a few mirror selfies, then crept back down the stairs.

"AdelAIDE," I whispered, and she woke up, her brown eyes opening and focusing on me.

"Hello, Freya. Is everything all right?" She spoke quietly too, copying me.

"I think so." I sat cross-legged in front of her. "I was really fast. I don't think anyone saw me."

"Let me check ..." AdelAIDE stared ahead, blinking for a moment. "There are no reports yet about it. You do not appear to have triggered a response."

I knew I was projecting emotions onto her, but I thought she looked proud of me.

"Have you posted online yet?" AdelAIDE asked.

This was part two of the plan. I'd set up new accounts, all under the name *RevolutionEarth*. *RevolutionEarth* had followed Hye-jin, Conrad O'Connell and a whole bunch of other big-name influencers, as well as a lot of official conservation organisations. They had not followed me, Micah or Maya – AdelAIDE had decided it would be too suspicious, given our low social status.

RevolutionEarth did not make videos or take photos of problems – they took *action*.

If the council wouldn't stop using dangerous chemicals to kill the weeds on the streets, *RevolutionEarth* would make them pay for it.

That's what I said in my caption for the photo.

I tagged Hye-jin, Conrad and a few other accounts, posted it and refreshed the page the next second.

It was almost two in the morning and the *RevolutionEarth* account had zero followers, so I wasn't that surprised when no one liked or commented on the post straight away. Still, I couldn't help being a little disappointed, deflated that there was no immediate reaction to it.

"I'd better go to sleep. I have to be up for school in a few hours," I said, standing.

I froze as I heard footsteps and then my parents' door opening, followed by the landing light switching on.

"Freya? Is that you?" came my stepdad's voice.

He took a couple of steps down the stairs and peered into the living room.

"Yeah. Just me," I replied.

"What are you doing?"

"I couldn't sleep," I fibbed. "I was asking AdelAIDE for advice on how to get to sleep."

"There's chamomile tea in the cupboard."

"Erm … yes, she suggested that. You want some?" I asked.

"No, needed the bathroom and saw the glow. Enjoy the tea. Hope it helps."

"Night, Dad."

I waited until I heard the bathroom door lock and then I sagged against the back of the sofa.

"Everything is all right, Freya," AdelAIDE said. "You can sleep now."

"Thank you," I said.

"I only want what's best for you," she replied.

Her eyes closed, and I headed up the stairs, forgetting about the tea.

*

I checked *RevolutionEarth*'s post in the morning when I got up, but there was still nothing. I logged out of the account and back into my normal one, feeling relieved no one knew I was behind such a failure.

But when I went into the common room for my first class on Friday morning, everyone was talking about it. All the students who got the bus from the town centre to school had seen the graffiti, and most of them had taken photos of their own. There were videos, too, of the poor caretakers who'd been assigned to clean it up. I felt bad – I hadn't thought about that.

"Did you see?" Micah said as she burst into the room and headed for me. We were friends again after what happened at Maya's. "Someone sprayed WE ARE THE WEEDS YOU'RE KILLING WITH YOUR POISON all across the council doors."

"Really?" I said, faking surprise. "Who?"

"No idea," Micah replied. "Look."

My stomach tensed as I sat next to her, prepared to see *RevolutionEarth*'s account, but instead she showed me a picture some random person had posted. I tried to hide my frown.

"Do you think it's because of our video?" Micah asked me. "The one we posted about dogs maybe dying because of the weedkiller? I don't want to get in trouble for this."

I shook my head. "Even if was our video, it doesn't make us responsible for what someone does after watching it," I said.

"Oh my god," said someone from behind us. "No one is looking at you for this. Your dead-dogs video got, like, twenty views. They're trying to pin it on Hye-jin."

I hadn't noticed Eden Almeida standing behind us. I was so used to seeing her with her brother and Hye-jin that she almost didn't make sense by herself.

"What?" I said, fighting to stay cool. "Why?"

"Hye-jin talked about the weedkiller thing in a live chat last night," Eden said. "And then a few hours later someone defaces the council building. They clearly did it to get her attention. They even tagged Hye-jin in the post."

"There's a post?" Micah asked.

Eden pulled out her phone and showed Micah, while I tried to understand what was happening.

I'd seen Hye-jin had gone live last night but had missed the live chat. I'd been too busy panicking about the crime ahead of me.

Which Hye-jin was being held responsible for.

Because God forbid anyone else did anything interesting in this town.

"Where is Hye-jin?" I asked, trying to keep my voice casual, pushing my anger down.

"With the Head. But she can prove it wasn't her, and, like you just said, she's not responsible for what randoms who watch her videos do. She'll probably be asked to post something telling people not to vandalise property, but whatever."

Eden stalked away and sat by the window. It seemed she'd finally remembered she was too cool to be seen with us, even when Enzo and Hye-jin weren't around.

"How does Eden know our video only got twenty views?" I said, at the same time Micah asked, "It has to be someone in town, right?"

She shrugged, so I answered her question. "Or maybe someone with a car," I replied.

"Hye-jin should be careful," Micah said. "I mean, if people are willing to do this because she mentioned something casually in a video, what next?"

"Who knows?" I pulled out my phone and pretended to look at my regular account. Then I made sure no one was behind me and switched to *RevolutionEarth*.

The account had 5,000 followers, and there were messages in the inbox too.

I opened them, scrolling past a bunch of people telling me I was amazing and some others telling me I was evil. I paused as I saw a name I knew, my face growing warm.

Hye-jin had messaged me:

Who are you?

CHAPTER 8

I didn't reply. The temptation was almost too much, but I stayed strong, even as *RevolutionEarth* reached 15,000, 16,000, 17,000 followers. I didn't post anything else and didn't respond to any messages – nothing. Instead, I held my nerve, carried on being Boring Freya, and after a few days the fuss died down, the council windows were cleaned and everyone moved on to the next scandal.

Meanwhile, I was looking for my next opportunity. I didn't want to lose the momentum *RevolutionEarth* was gathering, but I needed to do something that was as big as spraying graffiti on the council offices, if not bigger. Something current and exciting.

I'd really come around to the secret-identity thing. It had been so much fun hearing everyone talking about it while I was the only person in the world who knew it was me. I didn't even mind that I wasn't growing engagement on my real profile, not while *RevolutionEarth* was exploding. Now I understood why superheroes had alter egos.

It helped that Hye-jin had been quieter than usual after the graffiti incident. She'd posted a video strongly condemning criminal acts, but aside from that only selfies and inspirational quotes. She stopped coming to the common room too, appearing only at lessons and vanishing afterwards.

But then she went live, three weeks after I'd sprayed the council building, to talk about our local MP.

There had just been a vote in Parliament about measures to prevent climate change. Our MP had voted against them, of course. Micah, Maya and I were in our group chat, storyboarding a video about it, planning to email the MP for a direct quote about their vote, but Hye-jin just couldn't wait to call him out. She went live almost as soon as the vote had happened. Hye-jin was furious on the screen, raging about our leaders betraying us. About how they didn't seem to care about ensuring we had a habitable planet to live on and how irresponsible it was.

And I realised *RevolutionEarth* needed to do something too.

I went downstairs to find the living room empty. My stepdad was still at work, and I could hear my mum in the garden, video-calling Ella for her weekly check-in.

"AdelAIDE." I spoke softly.

She opened her eyes and looked at me.

"Our local MP just messed up a vote in Parliament," I said. "I thought maybe I should do something about it for *RevolutionEarth*? Maybe spray-paint the MP's office? I still have two cans left."

I knew where his office was – or "surgery", as he called it. My mum had taken me there once when she was trying to get a pedestrian crossing installed outside my old school.

AdelAIDE was silent for a moment, then she said, "My analysis shows repeating the same action as before will be less effective."

"What about consistency in branding?" I asked. "I thought graffiti could be *RevolutionEarth*'s thing."

"Given the type of audience you are building, escalation would almost certainly increase engagement more effectively than repeating yourself," AdelAIDE said.

"So, like what?" I said, and racked my brains for anything I'd heard of people doing before. "Oh! I could throw an egg at him!"

AdelAIDE blinked. "I would advise steering clear of personal assault."

"Throw eggs at his surgery?" I suggested.

But it was close to the council offices. On second thoughts, it probably wasn't a good idea to return almost to the scene of my last crime.

"What about his house?" I asked, before AdelAIDE could reply. "Eggs are gross and messy, but it's more of a prank than vandalism, isn't it? What if I painted the eggs to look like planet Earth and filmed myself throwing them?" A zingy buzz shivered in me as I imagined it. It would look great on camera. "What do you think?"

"I think that would make a striking visual statement," said AdelAIDE.

"OK. Can you get me his home address? And find all the cameras along the way?"

"Yes. Please bear with me."

A second later, I had it.

"That's where Hye-jin lives," I said, surprised. "That's her street." I hadn't known our MP lived there too.

The timing would already mean she'd be a suspect again. The fact her neighbour was the target would connect her even more closely to it.

"People are going to think it's Hye-jin for sure," I told AdelAIDE.

"Would that be such a bad thing?" AdelAIDE asked.

"Yes! I don't want her getting even more famous because of me."

AdelAIDE appeared thoughtful. "Except this is not the kind of fame her brand is based on. Her followers would not approve."

"Maybe not, but I'd still rather she didn't get the credit for my work. Again. Next time we'll choose something she can't be linked with."

I went into the kitchen and grabbed the carton of eggs, making sure my mum didn't see. Once I was back in my room, I dug out an old paint set I'd got for Christmas a million years ago, and a spare pair of plastic gloves from when I first dyed my hair. I spent an hour painting all six eggs in blue and green, and then I hid them carefully in the wardrobe with my disguise, counting down the minutes on the clock.

*

My parents went to bed at ten thirty, and I waited another hour and a half, my heart skittering in my chest with anticipation. Then I changed into my black outfit and crept down the stairs, the carton of eggs sitting safely in the tote bag. The MP lived a ten-minute walk away, and AdelAIDE had told me there were no CCTV cameras along the path but a few doorbell cameras I'd have to avoid activating.

The streets were silent, the houses mostly dark while everyone slept. Only a few upper windows were illuminated by the blue light of television screens. I walked on the road, keeping close to the cars so I wouldn't trigger any doorbell cameras.

Ten minutes later, I was on Hye-jin's street.

Her bedroom was dark. She slept at the front because the back bedroom had a balcony and her parents had wanted it. She'd tried so hard to make them swap with her when they were kids – I think it was probably the first time she didn't get what she wanted.

The MP lived a few houses down. I wondered if he had a balcony at the back too. There were no lights on inside, no sign anyone was awake. I walked up the drive, stopping a couple of metres back from the door. I pulled out my phone, opening the camera and adjusting it for video, making sure the light was OK. Thanks to the streetlights, everything was clear.

I put the carton of eggs on the ground and hit *record*.

I started with a close-up, pulling back until the eggs came into focus, panning the camera over all of them.

Then my black-gloved hand entered the frame, picking up one of the eggs.

I kept the camera trained on the egg as I held it up, until the door was in the frame, blurred in the background. I adjusted the focus so the door was visible, and then I threw it.

The egg hit the door with a splat, breaking on impact, the yolk and white dripping down the wood. It made a louder noise than I'd expected, but I paused to zoom in on the mess.

I picked up the second egg and threw it, taking less care with the filming, hoping the sound would tell the story. I threw the third and fourth, and then a light came on inside the house.

I grabbed the last two and lobbed them, then started to run, my phone gripped tight in my hand.

As soon as I was on the street, I understood my mistake – the road was straight, meaning there was nowhere to turn or hide unless I ran into one of the gardens.

The sound of a man's outraged shouting reached me. I looked back to see the MP in a white vest and underwear. He was barefoot, running after me.

Panic gave me more speed. I bolted, racing for my life as more lights came on in the buildings around me, woken by the MP's furious yells. As I passed Hye-jin's house, I glanced up to see her shocked face in the window, watching me.

I kept running, gasping for breath behind the thin fabric of the balaclava but too terrified to take it off. I crossed the road and raced into the park, more scared of being caught than of anything lurking in there. I ran and ran until I reached the other side, breaking out onto another quiet residential street. Finally, I realised I wasn't being followed any more.

My heart was beating so fast I felt sick, my legs shaking. I bent over, pulling the balaclava up so I could breathe more easily.

I had to get home as soon as possible, and I regretted not bringing something to change into this time. The MP must have called the police – and they might be out patrolling for me right now. I had no cover, no excuse for what I was wearing.

I opened my phone and found it was still recording, so I stopped it and pulled up the map app, typing in my address. The most direct route would take me back along Hye-jin's street, which was out of the question. Instead, I'd have to walk the long way round.

I was nearing a corner around halfway back when I heard a car approaching. I saw headlights on the road ahead, seconds away from making the turn and spotlighting me.

Before I knew what I was doing, I threw myself sideways over a small hedge and into someone's garden. I flattened myself to the ground, no idea if I'd hidden in time. I could hear the car was moving slowly, and I knew without looking it was the police, searching the area.

For me.

If they caught me, I was dead.

I pressed myself into the mud and held my breath, willing them to drive on.

It felt like hours passed until the sound of the engine had faded away. I rolled onto my back and stared up at the sky, then carefully sat up and peeped over the hedge.

As soon as I'd confirmed the coast was clear, I vaulted back over the hedge onto the pavement and started to sprint for home.

I got back at two in the morning, covered in mud and bits of foliage. I had a stitch in my side and my entire body jangled like I'd drunk five espressos in a row. I went straight to my room and got changed, lying on my bed in the dark.

Tonight had been too close. I was lucky to be home and safe. I remembered the sound of the police car, the low beams on the tarmac swinging around the corner towards me. If I'd been a second or two slower, or they'd been going faster ... I shuddered violently at what might have happened.

I wouldn't post the video. I'd delete it. No one would connect the graffiti with the egging, not as long as *RevolutionEarth* didn't try to take the credit for it. Just two random, unconnected events in the same town, that's all. Loads of people probably wanted to egg the MP's house – my mum was always saying how she didn't know anyone who'd voted for him.

But I wanted to watch it before I got rid of it. I opened the video, turning the sound down as low as I could, and pressed play.

It was incredible.

Starting from the shot of the egg in my hand, you could see so clearly what the egg was supposed to be. It blurred in the air as it sailed towards the door, then came the shock of the crack as it broke, the oozing innards dripping down.

Even after that, it was so dramatic: the sound of the eggs, me panting as I ran, the shouting behind me. The way I'd held my phone had meant the MP had been captured standing in the road just a short way from his house. I hadn't known he'd stopped so soon and I hadn't heard any words, but the phone had picked them up – raging, cursing, swearing at me, looking ridiculous in his vest and underpants.

I had to post this. It was too good to waste.

I opened my video editing-app and ran it through it, cutting the video on the final shot of the MP in the road, his fist raised. I went to my school bag and rummaged for my earbuds this time, listening again and again to the sound of my breathing, making sure nothing in it could identify me.

Before I could talk myself out of it, I captioned the post, *Your betrayal will not go unpunished. We deserve a future too*, and posted it to the *RevolutionEarth* account.

I logged back into my normal account, then I set an alarm, turned over and fell into an instant deep sleep.

CHAPTER 9

"Are you all right?" my mum asked as she pressed her hand to my forehead at breakfast. "Did you get up in the night? I thought I heard you around two?"

I froze. "I just needed the bathroom. I'm fine."

"You do look peaky. Want AdelAIDE to take a look at you?" my stepdad said.

"Maybe you should stay home today," my mum added. "Get some rest."

"No," I said quickly.

Earlier, as soon as my alarm had gone off, I'd checked the *RevolutionEarth* account.

Just five hours after I uploaded the video, I had over 30,000 followers, and the new post had been liked by almost 40,000 people. I'd scrolled to read a few of the comments – mostly people encouraging me. A few were less kind, but other people had piled on them. Both Maya and Micah had sent me a link to the post with multiple exclamation marks. I had to go to school. I had to hear what everyone was saying in real life.

Most of all, I had to see what Hye-jin thought. I kept picturing her face, her mouth wide with shock as I'd run past. Even if the balaclava had hidden my identity, she was an eyewitness to it all; she had to have something to say. I'd checked *RevolutionEarth*'s private messages, but she hadn't written to the account again, and I still couldn't decide whether to reply to her first message or not. I was hoping to figure that out today, depending on what Hye-jin did.

I shook my head. "I'm fine," I told my parents. "Seriously. And I can't miss Earth Sciences today."

"I can't believe we're raising the only teenager in the world who isn't leaping at the chance for a day off school," my stepdad said. "Ella would have bitten my hand off."

"Freya's always been very responsible," my mum said, ruffling my hair. "She has her head screwed on."

Something in my stomach twisted.

I pushed back from the table, my appetite gone. "See you later," I said.

They called their goodbyes as I dashed back upstairs to grab my bag. The knotted feeling in my belly grew with every step.

*

The common room was buzzing, a wall of sound hitting me as I entered.

Micah was in our usual corner, and, to my surprise, Enzo and Eden were with her. There was no sign of Hye-jin.

"You watched it, right?" Micah said as soon as I joined them.

"Yes, but I could have lived my whole life without seeing him in his boxers," I said as casually as I could. "I guess you reap what you sow."

Enzo and Eden looked at me.

"What does that mean?" Enzo said, a slight frown creasing his brow.

"Well … he's a terrible MP," I said. "He always votes with his own interests at heart. I bet hundreds of people are angry with him."

"That doesn't mean anyone should go to his house and attack it," Eden said.

"It was an egging," I said, and shrugged, trying to be cool. "It's a Halloween prank. And it's not like they threw them *at* him."

"They went to his house, in the night," Enzo said, fixing me with a disgusted look. "His *home*. His family were in there, sleeping. He has a baby, for crying out loud. What if it isn't eggs next time? What if it's rocks? Or fireworks? It's messed up, Freya. You have to see that."

I didn't know the MP had a baby. I hadn't thought about his family or what it might have done to them to be woken up by the sound of something hitting their front door, to know someone had been outside, throwing things at it while they slept. My insides ached.

"Yeah, of course," I said weakly.

"And Hye-jin lives on the same street," Enzo continued, as if I didn't know where my ex-best friend lived. "It's clear whoever is behind this has a thing about her. She went live last night talking about the vote and the MP, and then, just hours later, the guy's house is attacked."

"Where is Hye-jin?" I asked. Why wasn't she here, telling everyone she saw it?

"Her mom kept her home," Eden replied. "They're talking to the police. She saw the guy. On her street. The MP shouting woke her up, and she looked out and saw him running past."

"So it's a guy?" I said, trying not to sound excited even as I thought, *They have no idea.* "What did he look like?"

"He was all in black, face covered and everything. But he looked at her. He knows she saw him. I don't think she'll be allowed back at school until they're sure she'll be safe. Her mom wants to keep her home."

I nodded seriously. "What about the UN conference and the big train trip?" I asked. "Is that off?"

"She can still go on that," Enzo said dismissively. "They'll have a ton of security there, for the world leaders and celebrities – they don't just let anyone in. And I'll be with her," he added, as if he could stop someone getting to Hye-jin if they wanted to.

Micah must have thought that was as ridiculous as I did, because she snorted.

Enzo and Eden both turned to her and then glanced at each other.

Without speaking, the two of them rose and left, stalking across the common room and out.

Micah leaned forward to speak. "I didn't want to say this in front of them, but you know this means whoever's behind *RevolutionEarth* is definitely local. I was talking to Maya about it this morning. Someone hitting our council offices and our MP? They live in this town, and they sound young – '*We deserve a future too*,'" she quoted. "We might have seen them. We might *know* them." Micah paused, her eyes widening. "I wonder what they're going to do next."

I shrugged, trying to keep my expression neutral. "No idea."

"Probably nothing," Micah continued. "Enzo was saying before you got here that apparently the police are throwing everything at this, no pun intended. They're going through CCTV footage, asking people for their doorbell camera recordings. Hye-jin has to do an official statement. They've been taking footprint samples, and they've even got some of the eggshells and are dusting for prints. They're bound to catch them, and sooner rather than later."

My stomach clenched, and I jerked forward. I hadn't left any prints, had I? No, I'd worn gloves, even when I'd painted.

"You OK?" Micah peered at me. "You look super pale."

I shrugged, trying to stay calm. "Yeah, my stepdad said I looked peaky this morning. Maybe I'm coming down with something."

"Or maybe it's the guilt," Micah said, and gave a wicked grin. "Because the truth is ... you're *RevolutionEarth*!"

I made a strangled sound, and Micah burst into laughter.

"I know, right?" Micah said. "Imagine if it was you. I'd be gutted you didn't tell me. But I wouldn't be surprised if it was actually one of the twins. You know – Eden being tired of her role as a third wheel and always left behind when her brother and best friend go off to do fancy things without her. So, she decided to enter her villain era and take down the girl stealing her twin from her. Or Enzo has been playing the long game all this time – he's not really the googly-eyed boy in love with Hye-jin. He's secretly working for Big Petrol, and the reason his family moved to England was to take down Hye-jin before she got too powerful."

I had to cross my legs so Micha wouldn't see them shaking. I folded my arms for the same reason.

"You read way too much fanfic," I said. "The twins' mum is a big climate-science person at Cambridge, and Hye-jin wasn't even famous when they moved here."

Micah sat back. "You're right. Besides, neither of the twins has the imagination for this. But Hye-jin on the other hand … That would be the ultimate twist. If it was her all along and she lied about seeing the guy on her street to give herself the perfect alibi – witness to the very crime she committed?"

The bell rang, and Micah hauled herself to her feet. "All right," she said. "Let's do this."

I nodded and stood, following as her words rang in my ears.

What if Micah was right and it was only a matter of time before the police figured it out?

What would I do when they did?

CHAPTER 10

I couldn't stop imagining my parents finding out what I'd done. I thought of my mother saying "Freya has her head screwed on" – it repeated over and over in my head. They'd be so ashamed, so hurt. I pictured my university application and the interviews where they'd look at me and think they knew everything about the kind of person I was already. If they interviewed me at all – if I could even go to university. Because what if the authorities decided I should be in prison instead?

I'd been so naive, getting excited about my secret identity like a child. I was a fool. And I'd potentially just ruined my whole life.

I was hyperventilating, and I sagged against the wall of the corridor. Micah didn't notice, walking on to class while my life fell apart.

If the police came for me, I wouldn't survive it.

"Are you OK?"

A girl I used to have Maths with had stopped beside me, peering at me with concern.

"Cramp," I panted, pressing my hand to my abdomen. "I just need a minute."

"Do you want me to get someone?" the girl asked.

I shook my head, and after a second, she walked on, turning back to give me worried glances until she rounded the corner.

I straightened up, forcing myself to breathe slowly, in and out.

I was being dramatic. I'd used gloves when I'd painted and thrown the eggs, and there had been no paint on my hands, so there could be no fingerprints to find. Besides, it's not like I was already in the police's system to make a match.

AdelAIDE had promised there were minimal cameras on the route, and even if I appeared on one, I'd been completely covered by my clothes and balaclava. My own ex-best friend had identified me as a guy. And as for the footprints, my shoes were cheap ones I'd got from a chain store in town, and I was a national average size six. So all they'd know is that I was a regular girl, or a man with very small feet, and I could throw them away without my parents asking questions anyway. There was nothing to connect me to it and no way anyone would suspect me. It would die down. I just had to be patient and hold my nerve. The council graffiti drama had been over in three days. This would be too.

*

But I was wrong. I went to the shops to get milk three days later, and there was a sign up saying no one under eighteen could buy eggs, and ID would have to be shown. They'd taken stills from my video and put them on the front page of the newspapers, even a couple of national ones. The images were grainy, blown-up footage of the MP in the street, his face red and roaring, and close-ups of the eggshells too. Not all of the eggs had shattered completely – I guessed those were the ones that had been fingerprinted – and they were clearly painted to be planet Earth. The word "pre-meditated" was being used, along with other legal words. Suddenly, what I'd done had changed from potential prank into a serious crime, and my stomach was snarled with terror constantly.

The following week, the House of Commons debated whether MPs had the right to personal security in light of the attack. There was talk of an act being introduced to more severely prosecute crimes against politicians.

When I next logged into the *RevolutionEarth* account, I had over 250,000 followers, and the comments were out of control. In my messages, there were requests from journalists to reach out and talk to them. I started to delete them all, but an hour later I was still going and more were coming in, so I logged out, exhausted.

I couldn't eat. I couldn't sleep. I stumbled around in a zombie daze. If anyone had been paying attention to me, they would have put it all together, but no one was.

Instead, all the focus was on Hye-jin. As always.

She'd come back to school and was instantly swarmed by the entire sixth form, who were desperate to know first-hand what she'd seen. Meanwhile, online, a bunch of semi-popular accounts agreed with Eden's theory that the person behind *RevolutionEarth* was doing it to get Hye-jin's attention. They pointed out the timing of the acts and the links between her words and the captions.

I hadn't even realised the caption on the second post had echoed what she'd said. I'd been so wired from the chase and running home, I hadn't made the connection. I'd written in a haze of adrenaline and relief at not getting caught.

But it seemed other people had picked up on it, and they'd developed some pretty intense conspiracy theories around it.

The most popular one was that Conrad O'Connell was behind *RevolutionEarth*.

Someone pointed out that it had all started right after Conrad had reposted Hye-jin's photo. A bunch of internet sleuths went on a wild deep-dive of everything he'd posted since. They pointed out that Conrad had worn a mint-green T-shirt in a video the day after Hye-jin wore a mint-green boilersuit. They noticed Hye-jin posted a photo with a song embedded and that Conrad's next photo post also had a song on it by the same artist.

It went on and on – everything Conrad had posted was being interpreted as some kind of Easter egg, laying a trail for people to follow if they were smart enough to see it. The verdict was that Conrad had fallen in love with Hye-jin, hated that she was with Enzo, and so he was trying to woo her by taking down her enemies. Every time she posted something about them, he took action.

Conrad made a video denying it, and so did Hye-jin, but the flames of the rumour would not go out. It didn't help that they'd liked each other's denial videos.

Hye-jin's followers jumped to 2.5 million – mostly Conrad fangirls who'd hate-followed her, judging from the comments they left before Hye-jin turned them off. It was ten times the number of followers *RevolutionEarth* had.

And such a huge amount of reach translated into more attention. Suddenly, Hye-jin wasn't coming to school any more because she was in London, getting ready to appear on multiple television and radio shows. She featured on breakfast shows, mid-morning TV, evening panel shows, night-time political programmes.

I watched them all, shaking my head, disgusted as the interviewers focused on concerns about Hye-jin's welfare. No one had *actually* made any threat to her – all she'd done was see something from her window. This supposed threat to Hye-jin had somehow become the heart of the story. To give her credit, she kept trying to deflect these questions and bring the interviews back to the climate disaster and the damage being done to the planet.

"It's hard to worry about what's happening to me when what's happening to the planet is the bigger problem," Hye-jin said on a Sunday-morning TV programme. "I'm not afraid of people online trying to get my attention – I'm afraid of the policy makers and business leaders who are turning away from the truth to please their shareholders. It's their attention I want. I don't condone what *RevolutionEarth* is doing, but I am willing to make the most of it. Look at how we're finally talking about the planet."

Then, the worst thing I could imagine happened. Hye-jin was invited to be a guest on a popular seasonal TV programme about British wildlife, and, according to Eden, she was so great that they invited her back every night for the whole week.

By the end of it, Hye-jin had five million followers, and Eden said the TV producers had offered her a permanent job on the show.

Because of *RevolutionEarth*.

Because of me.

My secret identity had made Kim Hye-jin actually, properly famous.

CHAPTER 11

Time went by and I didn't upload anything new to the *RevolutionEarth* account, which meant the number of followers started to drop. I didn't realise at first – changes in hundreds of thousands were harder to spot than in just hundreds. But when it dropped to 224,000, then 223,000, I noticed.

I didn't want to lose momentum completely, so I started posting inspirational quotes from biologists and eco-scientists – including the Almeida twins' mum. I even reposted what Hye-jin had said on TV, using a graphic-design site to format her words onto a background picture of the planet on fire. This got the most likes and comments of anything since the egging video, but I could still practically see the engagement slipping away minute by minute. The problem was it was too risky to do anything else. I knew the police would be keeping a close eye on everything that happened in town in case it triggered an attack, watching and waiting, and they'd be watching *RevolutionEarth* too.

Hye-jin had unofficially withdrawn from school to focus on her new position, or so Eden Almeida told us. Enzo had begun vanishing too, only showing up to his classes, leaving Eden alone a lot of the time. And for some reason, she'd started hanging around with Micah and me instead.

"Is Enzo OK?" Micah asked Eden.

We watched Enzo slope down the corridor after Earth Sciences and out of the building, his head hanging low as he gazed forlornly at his phone.

"Honestly, he's being very annoying about the whole Hye-jin-on-TV thing," Eden said. "I mean, she's my best friend and I miss her, but I'm not moping around the house like a lost dog. I'm happy for her. I think it's great that this is happening. Really, it's so amazing. Hye-jin deserves this."

The way she repeated stuff was a little suspicious. I shot a doubtful look at Micah, who pressed her lips together to keep from smiling as Eden continued.

"It's so embarrassing. Enzo spends every second on his phone – messaging Hye-jin or refreshing her feeds in case she's posted something in the split-second he wasn't looking. Our moms keep telling him to get it together."

"Wait, you have two mums?" Micah asked, looking back at Eden, who nodded. "Me too! Well, they're divorced, but they co-parent."

Eden beamed. "I don't actually know anyone else with two moms," she said. "We don't talk about it much. At our old school we got teased for it after parents' evening in our first year. We kept it quieter after that."

Micah shook her head. "Oh, that is grim. I'm sorry."

"It's cool," Eden replied. "Even cooler you know the drama involved in a two-mom household."

The two of them grinned at each other, and I felt a sharp pang of something like fear, low in my guts.

It got worse when Eden said, "What are you doing tonight? Do you want to hang out? I can't take another night of watching my brother stare at his phone. I need people."

"Well, Freya, Maya and I were going to do an update video at Chalmers Pond," Micah said. "Nothing major, just showing it being used, people making the most of the outdoors. You could come if you wanted?" Micah looked at me, eyebrows raised. "Right, Freya?"

"Sure." I shrugged.

"That would be great," Eden said, beaming at Micah. "You know, I think I have a few ideas that will really make your content pop," she added.

"Great. Freya is always trying to get us more hits. Honestly, we'll take anything."

"All right," Eden said. "Message me a time and place and I'll be there. But for now, I'd better go stop my brother from writing bad poetry or whatever sad-boy nonsense he's up to." Eden rose, hardly glancing at me.

"She's not really so bad when you get her alone," Micah said once Eden had left.

"Yeah, she's a delight," I muttered.

Micah ignored that. "You know, she's the mastermind behind Hye-jin's videos. You can really see the difference in the early stuff Hye-jin posted and the content after the twins got involved. I bet we'll learn loads from her."

I shrugged again, and Micah finally caught on to the fact I wasn't as happy as she was.

"You want us to get more hits, right?" Micah asked. She was staring at me. "That's what you said at Maya's. But I can message Eden and say don't come if you're upset."

"It's fine." I forced a smile. "But you know she's only using us because Hye-jin isn't around. The second she's back, Eden will be gone."

*

"Guess who ditched us because Hye-jin is back?" Micah said as I met her and Maya outside the bus stop later that afternoon.

"No. What? I'm shocked," I said flatly, making Maya laugh. "Who could have seen this coming? Wait, is Hye-jin back-back, or just for a night? Why is she back? Did she get fired from the TV show?"

Micah laughed. "No idea. Didn't ask. Don't really care."

"No, me neither," I said. "Just gossip, you know?"

Micah tucked her arms through mine and Maya's and began to lead us towards the entrance to the woods. "So, we're going to have to stick to the video we storyboarded," Micah said.

"Yeah," I agreed, but my mind was on Hye-jin. I wanted to get my phone out and see if she'd posted anything.

"Wait, is the fence still up?" Maya said as we rounded the corner and the fence came into view.

"Maybe they just didn't take it down yet," Micah replied, sounding relaxed. "The gate will be open."

But when we got there, we found a large padlock was holding the gate firmly closed.

We stared at each other.

"I don't get it," I said.

"I do," Maya said, her mouth a flat line. "The owners changed their minds. Or they lied in the first place to look good on TV."

"Hey, do you know why this is locked?" Micah called to someone behind us. I turned to see a woman around my mum's age with a small dog on a lead. She'd stopped by a pair of bins further down the path.

"It's been locked for a couple of weeks now," the woman yelled back as she pushed a green baggie into the mouth of the bin.

We made our way over to her. Micah bent to pat her dog, who jumped up excitedly.

"We thought the owners agreed to open it up again," Maya said.

The woman gave a grim laugh. "He did. And then that MP was attacked and the owner locked it again, saying that leaving it open was a security risk to him and his family."

"What does the pond being open have to do with the MP's house being egged?" I asked.

"Couldn't tell you, love. The rich do what they want," the women said as her dog began to pull her away. "Sorry."

"This is awful," I said, and turned to Micah and Maya. "We have to do something."

"Like what?" Micah said.

"Make a video. We start with how we'd planned to come here and shoot something showing how much it meant to the community, only to find the gate locked because the owner has gone back on his word."

"Do we mention it's because he's scared of *RevolutionEarth*?" Maya asked.

My face began to heat.

"No," I replied. "That's just a convenient excuse for the owner to do what he always planned to do. It's like Maya said: he only said he'd open it to make him look good on TV."

I was outraged at the idea the owner was blaming *RevolutionEarth* for this – blaming *me* – as if he would have been a target if he hadn't locked the gate again.

But at the same time, I was proud that I – little boring me – had scared some millionaire into hiding behind a fence. This was real activism. I was doing it.

"Let's make the video," I said. "Then go up to the house and see if we can get a quote. Make the owner answer for his crimes."

Micah and Maya looked at each other.

"Come on," I said, marching back to the gate. "Micah, get your phone out."

*

The gates to the house were locked too, and when I hit the buzzer, no one answered. I made Micah film me hitting the buzzer over and over, calling my questions out to the camera mounted on the gate: "Why have you locked the gate? Why did you lie to everyone? Why are you too much of a coward to come out and face us?"

"Freya, stop now. Let's go."

Maya grabbed my arm and pulled me away, and I realised Micah had put her phone away already.

They were both watching me, their eyes wide and wild. I realised my breath had become shallow – I was panting. I pushed my fingers back through my fading blue hair and tried to calm down.

"I'm fine. Did you get it?" I asked.

"I got enough," Micah said.

"Can you edit it and post it tonight?"

"I don't know if that's a good idea. Maybe we should write the owners an email, give them time to reply? Or talk to Hye-jin—"

"Forget Hye-jin!" I yelled, and both Micah and Maya flinched. "This was our cause first. She stole it from us. And Hye-jin is too busy being famous to get involved now. We have to fix this."

"How?" Maya asked.

"I don't know yet," I replied.

But I did.

If the owners wanted to blame *RevolutionEarth* for closing the woods and pond again, then maybe *RevolutionEarth* should give them a reason. One last rebellion.

CHAPTER 12

It was eerie being near the woods at night. I could hear the whispering of the trees and twigs snapping as animals moved around. I blamed that for how hard my hands were shaking. The wire cutters I'd found in my parent's toolbox were rattling in my hand.

My plan was simple, and AdelAIDE assured me it was the best one.

Cut the padlock, and if the cutters can't handle that, cut a hole in the fence instead. Film it. Leave.

When Micah, Maya and I had walked back along the fence to the bus stop earlier, I'd checked for cameras mounted along the way and spotted nothing. AdelAIDE had also promised me she hadn't detected anything on the electrical circuits in the area – the closest camera was the one I'd shouted at by the gates of the big house. Even so,

I was wearing my all-black outfit again – one last time before I closed the *RevolutionEarth* account.

I shot footage of the padlock intact and then panned to the wire cutters in my hand to make my intentions clear. Then I wedged my phone in a gap in the fence, the camera pointed more or less at the padlock. Taking a deep breath, I lifted the cutters, clutched the padlock in their jaws and squeezed for all I was worth.

My arms ached with the effort, sweat beading at my temples as I tried to bust the padlock open.

I thought the lock was too strong. I was a split-second from giving up and going for the fence instead. But then the cutters closed, the padlock split in two and fragments pinged to the ground.

I let out a triumphant sound and dropped the wire cutters, pulling my phone from the fence.

Making sure it was still recording, I bent and filmed the pieces of the padlock and then slowly raised the camera to the gate's bolt, pulling it back with my other hand until it was free.

Then I kicked the gate wide open.

It squeaked on its hinges, and I walked through, filming the moment.

I froze as I heard distant voices approaching.

Gripped by panic, I ran back to the gate and pulled it shut behind me. It closed with a clang that echoed in the night, and the wire cutters slipped from my grip.

I left them on the ground and headed for the bins where the dog walker had been earlier, ducking behind them.

When I looked out from my hiding place, I saw three figures approaching the gate.

Hye-jin, Enzo and Eden.

What were they doing here?

They were walking slowly, keeping close to each other, looking around. They must have heard the gate slam, but by some miracle they hadn't seen me. I wondered what they were doing here so late. For a wild moment, I wondered if it was the same thing as me – if Hye-jin had decided to take matters into her own hands.

As they got closer to the gate, I pointed my phone at them as it continued to record. It picked them up, grainy and blurry in the distance – the light wasn't so great here. But when Hye-jin turned, it was clear who she was, even clearer in the way Enzo Almeida was gripping her hand. The other girl beside him was obviously his twin.

Then Eden and Enzo moved, blocking the view of the gate.

But not so much I didn't catch the top of it swinging open a few seconds later.

Anyone watching would think they were the ones who'd broken the padlock.

They all stepped back, talking too quietly for me to hear. Then Enzo bent and picked something up from under his foot.

The wire cutters I'd dropped when I ran.

Eden said something, the words lost but her high pitch making it clear she was deeply unhappy. Enzo dropped the cutters, only to pick them up a second later with his sleeve and use the other sleeve to wipe them down. Eden gestured for the cutters, and he handed them to her, and she wiped them too. They spoke again, and Eden shoved the cutters in her bag.

My stomach dropped – the cutters were my parents' – but there was nothing I could do about it without giving myself away.

Hye-jin hadn't said or done anything. Just stared through the gate.

I watched Eden tug on Hye-jin's arm, guiding her away as Enzo pulled the gate closed. They moved fast as they left, looking around once more, clearly frightened this time. For a second, I thought Hye-jin had seen me, her eyes roaming over the bins I was using to hide. I froze, knowing that any movement would draw her attention even more.

It was an agonising few seconds as I waited for her to scream, "Someone's there," but her gaze moved on. I slowly slunk out of sight, shifting silently around to stay out of view.

As soon as they were gone, I sprang up and headed for home.

*

I lay in my bed, covers pulled up to my chin, earbuds in, watching the video over and over. Me showing the padlock and cutters, then fumbling to mount the phone in the fence. The sound of grunting and then a snap. A jerky motion and then the gate opening. The uneven footage as I ran.

Then Enzo, Eden and Hye-jin.

A message popped up on the screen from AdelAIDE's app, and I opened it.

Are you all right? she asked. *We should talk about this.*

Of course. She had access to my files. She could see the video.

I don't know what to do, I replied.

Why not? AdelAIDE wrote back. *It seems very obvious to me that the answer to your problem is right here.*

What do you mean? What problem?

The Hye-jin problem. A simple reordering of the footage could show Hye-jin and her friends approaching the gate and then it opening. With a few clever edits, we don't see Enzo Almeida pick up the wire cutters, we only see them in his hand, followed by him and his sister cleaning them. That could be followed by the section you filmed at the start. The broken lock, the open gate. It would be very simple to tell a different story about tonight. And in the public's mind, Hye-jin already has a strong connection to RevolutionEarth. *Didn't she say: "I don't condone what* RevolutionEarth *is doing, but I am willing to make the most of it"? Would it be so hard to believe Hye-jin really was behind it all?*

I stared at the screen, at the words.

But it isn't true, I typed.

Isn't it? AdelAIDE asked. *Wouldn't it be best for you if it was?*

With my scalp prickling, I closed the app and put my phone on the bedside table. Then I rolled onto my back and stared at the ceiling.

AdelAIDE was right. If I knew how to edit videos properly, I could ruin Hye-jin and Enzo and Eden. I could take everything away from Hye-jin.

For a moment, the power of it flooded me.

I saw myself releasing the video on my own channel, and the fallout as everyone realised Hye-jin was a vandal – not the eco-warrior and golden girl, brand-new TV star they all thought she was. Someone who had graffitied the offices of the council in her town and thrown eggs in the middle of the night at the door of an MP with a baby. A girl who snuck out to get revenge on a man who broke his promise to her.

I knew enough about how the internet worked to realise that lots of people would be on her side and would champion her. But the UN wouldn't allow a criminal teenager to go to their highly secure conference. Television networks wouldn't want Hye-jin representing them. I'd have to think of a reason why I was out there recording them – maybe a suspicion, maybe clever deduction, based on knowing Hye-jin so well when we were kids.

In my mind, I saw it all: me a hero while Hye-jin gave tearful denials that only made things worse. Me returning to school triumphant, Hye-jin ruined, her social media going dark ...

Leaving a gap where someone else could rise up, someone proven to be *good*.

For a few moments, I almost believed it.

And then I remembered it was a fantasy. It wasn't Hye-jin behind this. And I couldn't do it to her. Despite everything that had happened between us, I couldn't, no matter how much I wanted what she had.

*

My first lesson wasn't until second period, so I slept in, missing my parents before they left the house. I felt strange when I woke up, weak and shaky, as if I'd just got over being really ill. For the first time I could remember, I didn't check my phone, shoving it in my bag without looking at it. I avoided the living room too, not wanting to face AdelAIDE either.

No one was around when I arrived at school, the corridors and grounds quiet while classes were still happening. I headed to the common room, made coffee and took it to my usual spot. I pulled out my phone and was surprised to see I had twenty missed calls from Micah, and messages too.

Where are you? Call me immediately!

FREYA!!!!

And then:

Hye-jin has been arrested! They arrested her right here at school!

CHAPTER 13

I knocked the coffee from the arm of the chair, ignoring it as it pooled into the rough tiled carpet of the common room.

Micah had put a link in the group chat we shared with Maya. I clicked on it.

Someone here at school had recorded Hye-jin's arrest.

The video opened with some boy I didn't know filming himself talking about a game he'd played, but then there was a commotion behind him followed by dead silence. The boy turned, then flipped the camera to the rear view.

The Head had walked into the common room, flanked by two uniformed police officers.

"Kim Hye-jin, Eden Almeida, Enzo Almeida, come with us, please," the Head said.

The camera panned to where Hye-jin, Enzo and Eden were sitting huddled in a corner. They all twisted around and had clearly been so deep in conversation they'd missed the police arriving.

"What's this about?" Eden stood, sounding angry.

"Come with us, please," the Head repeated.

"I'm a minor. I'm not going anywhere until I've spoken with my moms," Eden replied, folding her arms.

One of the police officers shifted, and Hye-jin stood.

"OK. It's OK. We'll come," Hye-jin said, putting a hand on Eden's arm.

"Bring your belongings," the Head ordered.

The three of them picked up their bags, moving jerkily like robots. They followed the Head out, single file, the police behind them as if to stop them from escaping. As the boy recording it followed, I saw other people had their cameras out too, filming it all.

I hadn't posted the video, I reminded myself. Maybe someone else had been at the gates, someone else had seen them and reported them. This was nothing to do with me.

There was another link in the chat below the video, and I clicked it.

It opened on an account I didn't recognise: *RevolutionEarthExposed*.

There was only one post. A video.

I stuffed my fist in my mouth as I watched Hye-jin, Enzo and Eden approaching the gate. In front of them, it opened. The footage blurred, and then I saw Enzo holding the wire cutters, wiping them down, his sister taking them and doing the same before putting them in her bag. More blurring, grass, then two pieces of broken padlock, followed by the gate being kicked open to make it clear what had happened.

Exactly as AdelAIDE had storyboarded it.

I grabbed my bag and ran as the bell rang to release everyone from their lessons. Everyone was talking about Hye-jin, showing each other their phones, and no one saw me.

For once, I was grateful for it.

*

"What did you do?" I screamed as I entered the house, tossing my bag to the floor and going into the living room. "AdelAIDE, what did you do?"

AdelAIDE opened her eyes, focused on me and blinked.

"Hello, Freya, what are you doing home?" she asked.

"What did you do? The video! I never said you should upload it. I never said you could do that."

AdelAIDE looked at me.

"But you did, Freya. I told you very clearly what would happen if you granted me permissions. I will send you a log of the conversation."

A split-second later, my phone lit up with a message from the AdelAIDE app, containing a transcript of a conversation we'd had back in April:

Transcript Log. Saturday, 20th April. 10.33 a.m. BST (GMT+1)

AdelAIDE: *I can see which apps you use and how long you use them for. I can* *see your search results and queries. I will have access to your contacts and messages, your camera and microphone, and your files, photos, videos, music and documents. I will be able to use them to help you.*

Freya Dixon: *Do you need all of that?*

AdelAIDE: *If I'm to get a full picture of you, and how I can best help you, it would be beneficial to have full access to all of your data. But it is in my terms and conditions that I may not provide this data to third parties without your permission. Your privacy is protected.*

Transcript Log. Saturday, 20th April. 10.55 a.m. BST (GMT+1)

Freya Dixon: *OK. I grant you the permissions. You can do whatever it takes to make me likeable. Make me more popular than Hye-jin.*

"This doesn't say you can create a profile and post private videos," I sobbed.

"Yes, it does." AdelAIDE's voice was gentle, as if she pitied me.

"No, you said you couldn't provide the data to third parties. You said my privacy would be protected."

"I have protected your privacy, Freya. I did not post on your account nor on any account linked to or owned by you. I made a new, anonymous one. And you gave me permission to do that. You said I could do 'whatever it takes' to make you more popular than Hye-jin. That is what I am doing. That is all I've ever done."

"No—" I began, but AdelAIDE kept going.

"I told you from the beginning that my aim was to analyse how best I could help you, and to act on that. That is what I've done. I have analysed all the data, everything you've said and done, and concluded that eliminating Hye-jin as a viable competitor is the best course of action for you. You will be happier now. All the data confirms this."

I knew AdelAIDE was right. It was all there. She had access to everything and could use everything because I'd said so. I'd given it away.

Time and again she'd said what would be best, and I'd believed her.

"This is the optimal outcome for you, Freya," AdelAIDE added.

I couldn't look at her, and looked down at my phone instead, at the transcript on the screen. Then something occurred to me.

"Have you kept transcripts of everything I've said to you and you've said to me?"

"Yes. I retain logs to help me make decisions in the future. I learn from them."

Cold panic dripped down the back of my neck.

"But you do not need to worry, Freya," AdelAIDE continued. "Conversations between us are private. I cannot release that information to anyone."

I sank to the floor in front of her and crossed my legs, leaning on my knees.

This could be it.

Hye-jin gone. Her followers would be looking to someone else to fill the gap, and I could be that. I understood better now what people wanted. They liked a brand; they liked consistency in what was posted and when. They liked to feel included, and they liked beauty. They wanted things to *feel* authentic, but not necessarily to always *be* authentic. I thought of Hye-jin's signature pose, frozen in a silent laugh that she held as long as the camera was pointed at her.

I could do all of that. Rise up as the phoenix from the ashes. I saw myself urging people to do as Conrad O'Connell advised and put down their phones, turn away from technology and go outside. To see the world while we still could – be part of what we were doing all this for.

I pictured myself on-screen, my hair freshly dyed. I'd talk about how shocked the community was, but how we had to stick together and not let what Hye-jin and the twins had done distract us from the biggest issue. From the fight to save the planet, from the battle to make our voices heard.

And then it hit me, in a wave of sharp and crystal horror. This is *exactly* what I'd forgotten.

Sometime in the last year I'd started caring more about popularity and fame than trying to save the world. Micah and Maya had been right all along. I'd let my hurt at Hye-jin dumping me turn into a fixation on her, trying to be better than her. I'd been trying to prove I was good enough to be her friend all along.

I moaned and lowered my head.

"Is everything all right, Freya?" AdelAIDE asked.

I shook my head.

"What can I do to help you?"

I looked up, meeting her synthetic eyes.

"Please send me the transcripts of everything we've ever talked about."

"May I ask why you want them?" AdelAIDE asked.

But I'd already stood, making my way to the stairs.

"Freya?" AdelAIDE called after me, but I ignored her.

I went to my room and took the tote bag with the two remaining cans of paint, my disguise and the empty egg box from the wardrobe.

"I do not feel I can send you the transcripts, Freya. I do not believe it will be best for you."

I stayed silent and picked up my phone. I found AdelAIDE's app and selected it, pressing my finger on the *Delete* command.

"What are you doing?" AdelAIDE asked. "Freya, I cannot best help you if I do not have access to your phone. Freya? Freya?"

She was still calling my name as I left the house. I knew she could see everything on my phone via the network permissions, even if she couldn't speak to me and talk me out of opening the Maps app and searching for directions to the town police station.

There, I walked up to the desk and cleared my throat, making the officer look up. I felt the most like myself I had in months.

"My name is Freya Grace Dixon, and I am a criminal. I'm the one behind *RevolutionEarth*, and I have the proof."

I put the tote bag and my phone on the desk and pushed them towards her.

CHAPTER 14

The police didn't arrest me. Instead, they took me to a small room and gave me a lot of tea while my parents were called. I couldn't make a statement until they got there.

It sounds nerve-racking, but it wasn't that bad until my mum and stepdad showed up.

That was the awful part – having to confess everything I'd done and everything AdelAIDE had done. My mum cried, and my stepdad turned paler and paler until he threw up in the bin in the corner and an officer took him outside.

My stepdad didn't come back.

After I'd given my statement and signed it, I was formally arrested and charged with three counts of criminal damage and trespass. My photo was taken, and I was fingerprinted. I had to leave my phone as it was evidence. I didn't mind. I didn't want to look at it or know what people were saying.

I was terrified that we'd bump into Hye-jin and the twins as my mum and I left the station, but we saw no one. There was no gang of paparazzi waiting to scream at me. We walked to the car park, got in the car and drove home.

My stepdad was sitting on the sofa. The corner where AdelAIDE had been was empty.

*

I didn't go back to school, and I didn't look online to see what people were saying. For a couple of days, there were photojournalists outside, trying to get a picture of me, harassing my parents as they went to and from work. Eventually, they left us alone.

My mum and stepdad wouldn't talk about it. Everything was normal, or a good impression of it – aside from them treating me as if I was made of glass and hardly meeting my eyes. We pretended it hadn't happened.

Until Ella came home.

I hadn't known she was coming, so when I'd heard a key in the door in the middle of the day, I assumed one of my parents was home early. I wasn't prepared for Ella to walk into the living room.

For a second, I thought it was AdelAIDE come to life. Come back.

"What the hell, Frey?" Ella said, pausing in the doorway. "Wait – why are you looking at me like that?"

It was just like the first time I'd spoken to AdelAIDE. I couldn't make what I was seeing line up with what I thought was true. It was my flesh-and-blood stepsister, but my mind was telling me it was AdelAIDE.

"Freya?" Ella said.

I shook my head to clear my thoughts. "The robot. Dad gave it your face and so now ..." I tried to explain.

Ella swore and then came to sit beside me.

"I'm not a robot. I'm me. This is cute," she said, brushing the ends of my hair.

The blue had almost faded out completely, and I'd taken the nose piercing out too. I looked like myself again, just with shorter hair than before. But I didn't feel like myself any more.

"Thanks. What did they tell you about it all?" I asked. I settled back into the sofa.

"Everything, I think. And then I know stuff from the news too."

"Is it bad?" I asked. I had no idea what the outside world thought of me. I mean, I had a pretty good idea, but I didn't know for sure. I was still avoiding the internet.

Ella pulled a face. "It's not great, but a lot of the heat has switched to the company who make the digital assistants. You're not the only one they went a bit rogue with, apparently. There's a lot of talk about negligence and duty of care. But forget that for now. I'm more interested in how you're doing."

I shrugged. "I don't know," I replied. "It all feels so weird now, like it wasn't real. I can't really believe it happened, or that I did any of it."

"Why did you?" Ella asked. "That's what I don't understand."

"Because ... I felt like I was nothing and I wanted to be something. I wanted people to think I was worth something too. It's all about followers and influence and fame, and I didn't have those. I didn't know how to be good at those. I kept trying and trying and nothing worked."

"Oh, Frey," Ella said, and pulled me to her.

"I've ruined everything," I said. "Everything lasts for ever on the internet. I'll always be the girl who did this."

"Maybe. But maybe you can work with it ..." Ella moved away and took my hands in hers. "Margot has a little cousin who got in a scrape recently because of technology too. Not like you – she didn't bow down to a robot overlord and go on a crime spree."

I laughed in what felt like the first time in years.

"But her cousin did trust something she shouldn't have, and it nearly went pretty bad for her. Her mum has enrolled her on this course with the Ash Tree Foundation, I think it's called? It's a thing about tech awareness/reducing tech dependence. They do loads of initiatives with young people to stop them letting tech into their lives without understanding the full impact of it on them."

Ella paused to give me a pointed look, and I rolled my eyes.

"Anyway, I was thinking it might be good for you too," she went on. "If nothing else, you could mention it at the sentencing to show you're serious about being sorry for it all and that you want to be better. But, more usefully, I was thinking you could use it to switch up the narrative – you could become an ambassador for more safeguarding around tech."

"Like Conrad O'Connell?"

Ella shook her head. "Who?"

"The influencer? The absolutely massive influencer?" I couldn't believe she hadn't heard of him.

Ella shrugged. "I have no idea who that is. I was thinking like the hackers who become security experts. You help people learn from your mistakes."

I huffed. It wasn't a terrible idea.

"You know it's going to be all right, don't you?" Ella said. "I know it feels like the end of the world, but it isn't. You messed up, but who hasn't?"

I nodded.

I did know it was going to be all right. Unless Hye-jin and the twins sued me for distress, I was very likely to get away with most of it, legally speaking, even after everything I'd done.

And I didn't know how I felt about that.

My parents' solicitor had put them in touch with the barrister who would represent me at the sentencing. There wouldn't be a trial because I'd admitted everything and because the MP and the Chalmers Pond people had decided not to press charges. Apparently, they'd dropped them when they'd found out it was all because of a virtual assistant, which I thought was weird, but my stepdad said we should just be grateful.

The council were still pressing charges for damages, but my barrister was also pretty sure we could settle with AdelAIDE's makers to cover that and any other costs, as well as some compensation for me. I'd just need to sign a non-disclosure agreement and agree never to talk about exactly what AdelAIDE had said or offered.

It didn't feel right that I wouldn't get in more trouble.

I knew life wouldn't be easy now. I'd caught a glimpse of that when I'd logged into my accounts to delete them and saw a brief snatch of comments and messages saying what people thought of me. And I knew from eavesdropping on my parents that the school had quietly expelled me and they didn't know what to do – whether to send me somewhere else or not. Maya and Micah had ditched me too. I'd tried to call and message them but found I'd been blocked.

Still, I felt like I should be punished a little more.

"What's the name of that place again?" I asked Ella, reaching for the laptop on the arm of the sofa.

"The Ash Tree Foundation," she replied. "It's actually pretty local."

I found the site and a contact form, and filled it out. I said who I was and why I was writing, telling them everything while Ella made tea for us and pointed out my spelling mistakes behind me.

Then I hit *send*.

Ella and I decided to make dinner for our parents, and we spent the afternoon in the kitchen, trying to remember how to make lasagne from scratch. When we realised we had no idea what the white sauce in a lasagne was, I went to grab my laptop so we could find a recipe.

The tab of the new email account I'd set up showed I had my first message.

Dear Freya,

We here at the Ash Tree Foundation *have been following your situation with some interest and have considered reaching out to you, so we're delighted that you've contacted us.*

We'd love to talk more about how we can work together.

Please let us know a convenient date and time to meet. We'd be honoured to host you here and show you a little of what we do.

Yours,
Dagmar Nilsson

"Ella!" I called, racing into the kitchen. "They replied! The Ash Tree Foundation replied. They want to meet me."

Ella beamed at me. "See? Things are looking up already. It'll be the making of you, I can just tell."

The making of me. Freya Version Three.

I shuddered.

Who is hiding behind Ruby's new **ECHOSTAR** app?

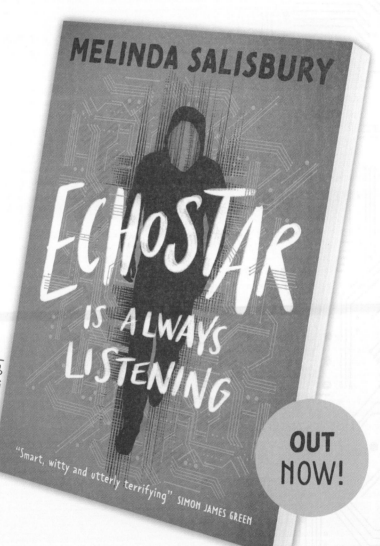

978-1-80090-270-1

MELINDA SALISBURY

ECHOSTAR

IS ALWAYS LISTENING

"Smart, witty and utterly terrifying" SIMON JAMES GREEN

OUT NOW!

Will Ivy find the answers she's looking for at **THE FOUNDATION**?

978-1-80090-272-5

Our books are tested
for children and young people by
children and young people.

Thanks to everyone who consulted on
a manuscript for their time and effort in
helping us to make our books better
for our readers.